From Colonial Ceylon to Down Under

Christine Hand

From Colonial Ceylon to Down Under

Short stories

Acknowledgements

Some of these stories have been published previously:
'Pie in the Sky', in *Adelaide Magazine*, 2020
'Escorted to Death', in *Adelaide Magazine*, February 2021
'A Hands-on Approach', in *Reedsy*, January 2022

Thanks

Special thanks to Judi Carr, Kelly Lyons, Kath Harrison, Rebekah Brammer and Alex Hand for their ongoing support in reading, critiquing and making suggestions for improvement. A very special thank you to Harriet Milks for her empathy, optimism, and persistent words of encouragement that have helped me along this journey. Last but not least, a big thank you to Stephen Matthews OAM for making this publication possible.

From Colonial Ceylon to Down Under: Short stories
ISBN 978 1 76109 446 0
Copyright © text Christine Hand 2022
Cover image: Yuri from Pixabay

First published 2022 by
GINNINDERRA PRESS
PO Box 3461 Port Adelaide 5015
www.ginninderrapress.com.au

Contents

To the memory of Alice White and Patrick

A Hands-on Approach

The waiter placed the tray of cakes on the table and went back to fetch the tea. Patti's was one of the very popular teashops in Colombo. It was where the three girls enjoyed meeting regularly.

'Utterly unbelievable! The traffic on the Galle Road is an absolute nightmare. It's taken me twice as long to get here today,' moaned Rita as she wiped the sweat off her brow with the flourish of a silk hanky. 'And all because of some sort of religious convention taking place in front of the Wellawatte market.' She showed her annoyance by engaging in battle with the chair before plonking herself down on it with a sigh. Rita did have some airs and graces about her and one of them was to make much of little, but she was very much a no-nonsense person.

'We've got a flyer about it,' chirped Manel as she rummaged through the contents of her handbag and pulled out the crumpled piece of paper. 'Tina and I thought it might be interesting to attend. It's on for the entire week. Look,' she said as she straightened it out for Rita to read, 'it's some sort of new-fangled evangelical ministry from the States and it's some local chap who's preaching…claims that he can heal on the spot. Of course, it's drawing crowds of people from all over Colombo and the rest of the country as well. Seems to be quite a sensation.'

Manel was in her mid-twenties, always quietly spoken. She was slender in build and generally preferred to remain in the shadow of her older sister, Tina. The three girls had known each other since school years.

Conversation while waiting for the tea to arrive revolved around all the gossip that the girls had to give and take. Manel gave eye signals to the other two to look towards her right. Sitting in the corner was a tired-looking woman with two little children. She was trying desperately to feed the baby on her lap while the older child, who looked around two, was demanding her attention with shrill cries while tugging at her arm and dress.

'Aren't you glad we aren't in that situation?' remarked Tina in a hushed tone. 'The poor woman can hardly manage those two and she looks pregnant with a third. God help her! Manel and I are glad marriage is not on our agenda,' said Tina.

Manel gave the woman a sympathetic smile as she caught her eye for a moment.

'I totally agree,' remarked Rita, looking at the woman with pity. 'Just imagine, she'd never have the time to meet with friends like we do or have any time to herself. How lucky we are to be independent!'

The tea arrived, and now the girls had other things to discuss.

'Let's see now…who's this preacher?' said Rita as she ironed out the pamphlet with her palm. 'Dennis Perera! No, it can't be the Dennis Perera I'm thinking of.' She screwed her face to scrutinise the small portrait inset. 'My God! It is him! I'll never forget those large, piercing eyes of his. This really is the same person. He lived next door to us and he got kicked out of school when he was just twelve. After that, he was in no end of trouble with the police; breaking and entering, burglary, car theft, you name it, he was involved. So now he claims to be a man of God! Yes, we must definitely attend to see what this chap is up to. Let's make it tomorrow. Are we agreed?'

'Yes, after what you've just said, I'm even more interested to hear what this "man of God" has to say,' remarked Tina.

Arriving at the scene the next day was an experience in itself. There was an immense throng gathering for the convention, which was housed under a large tent with loudspeakers fitted all around. The market stallholders were still busy packing up for the day; large piles of rubbish had yet to be collected. A strong aroma of roasted peanuts and ripe fruit – mangoes, durians and bananas – wafted around with the occasional breeze. It was the open-air market that was being used for the convention, and already the space appeared to be inadequate; such was the public interest and enthusiasm to hear this radical speaker whose fame was without a doubt, spreading far and wide. The girls felt increasingly uncomfortable as more and more people made their way in, pushing and jostling for a reasonable enough spot. Rita kept mopping the sweat off her brow every few minutes and Manel was never gladder that she carried that small fan in her handbag. The air inside the tent had become stale and oppressive, unbearable until the meeting got under way. When it did, they soon forgot the physical discomforts; the crowd focused with intent on the stage.

The voice boomed out from behind the podium. 'Hallelujah! Thank you, Lord, for saving a sinner like me. Thank you for washing away my sins. I was once a sinner, a lost soul. Yet you took me by the hand and washed me in the blood of Jesus Christ and I am now reborn! Thank you, Lord, hallelujah! We praise and give thanks to you, O Lord, Amen... Amen!'

As pastor Dennis's voice boomed through the loudspeakers, the audience swayed and swooned, mimicking his words. He in turn paused after each utterance, to hear their response, and ensure their participation.

'Praise the Lord.'

'Hallelujah.'

'Amen, thank you, Lord.'

'Wash me in the blood of Jesus Christ. Let me be reborn. Amen.'

This prologue was followed by a sermon like no other the three girls had ever heard. It homed in on the stories of Jesus healing the sick, making the blind man see, and enabling the lame to walk. The audience was tantalised, mesmerised; the sincerity injected into this sermon was compelling and utterly impossible to dismiss as fraudulent. This expectation, after all, was what the three friends had come to confirm, and now they were truly dumbfounded.

'My word, he certainly is one hell of a speaker,' said Tina. 'I never expected one of our countrymen to speak with such clarity and power.'

'I am totally and utterly impressed. I can hardly believe that I'm here listening to this guy speak this way. Let's move a bit closer to the front so we can see him better,' said Rita.

The girls squeezed their way towards the front and waited in anticipation.

Pastor Dennis had gone into a sort of trance, still vociferous but in a gentler, quieter tone. He was coaxing those who were infirm, whatever that infirmity might be, to have faith in God, mount the podium and ask for healing. Slowly but surely, five or six people made their way up. Together with two other pastors, they prayed, asking for forgiveness and cleansing. Then came the laying of hands on the sick individuals, one by one. Pastor Dennis then proceeded to ask each of them to testify about what had happened.

'I was blind in my left eye…but now I can see! It's a miracle, praise be to God! I can cover my right eye and I can see you and you…and you,' he said, pointing to the three pastors on the stage. 'And I can see all of you down there,' he said, pointing to the masses in front of him. 'Thank you, Lord, for healing me.'

'I have used these crutches for the last ten years when I lost the use of my right limb in a road accident. But look…I don't need my crutches any more. I can walk again!' The man threw his crutches on the stage and strode up and down the podium to demonstrate his mobility. He flung his arms up to praise the Lord and give thanks, as did the audience in happy bewilderment.

The faith healing was what the people had come for, and what they had witnessed had convinced much of the audience that Pastor Perera had delivered on his promise. Here was a genuine man of God, a man so blessed that they could really hope to have their ailments and disabilities disappear; all that was required was their faith, to allow him to lay his hands on them. Miracles were taking place in front of their very eyes! The fervour inside the tent was high. Emotive music blared out of the megaphones singing songs of praise; the audience caught on quickly and the sound built up to a thunderous crescendo.

An usher herded the newly healed to the rear of the podium, whence they presumably left and rejoined the audience to share their experiences. Rita astutely made note of this. She was determined to find out what was taking place backstage, and so it was that the three girls attended the convention yet again the next day.

'I know you say he was a terrible person, Rita, but people do change, and I'm convinced that Dennis has changed for the better,' remarked Manel.

'Rubbish!' said Rita. 'We're going to check this out again…properly.'

Arriving early the next day, they positioned themselves towards the side of the podium. It was the faith healing that the girls questioned.

They waited. The rejoicing over the healing ended, and the participants were being moved to the rear of the stage. The girls squeezed their way through the crowd towards the back of the tent.

'Tina! Watch your step. You're about to trip on that peg sticking out.'

'My heels are getting stuck in the mud,' wailed Tina.

'Shush, be quiet and watch. Listen, and try not to be seen,' said Rita in a sharpish voice.

They peered through the flaps of the tent into the back of the enclosure. An assistant had guided in three men and two women; he stood in front of them, monitoring the process. Another man sat at a table, counting out ten-rupee notes and stacking them up in neat piles. The five devotees were beckoned to line up in front of him. The first was handed a pile of notes which the man in charge counted out loud.

'This is only one hundred rupees. I was promised five hundred!' the recipient sounded indignant.

'Keep your voice down or you won't be getting anything,' said the other. 'You have not finished your job as yet. Remember, you must go out…mingle with the audience. Rejoice and praise the Lord, and remind them that you have been healed. They must get a positive message from you, and don't forget, you must be here tomorrow as well when the convention wraps up. That's when you'll get the rest of your money. And the same applies to all of you.' With that, he gave each their down payment and had them escorted out.

'Ah-ha, exactly what I thought,' whispered Rita jubilantly.

Manel and Tina seemed shocked and aghast. Was this really what was going on? They tiptoed round the side and left the show, leaving the gullible to enjoy it.

'I need a cup of tea badly,' said Manel. 'Let's go to Patti's.'

They trundled off to discuss this fresh but disturbing experience.

*

This was just the beginning of the evangelical movement in Colombo. It grew into a mass movement with exponential momentum. Island nations seemed particularly drawn by what the ministry offered, and people attended the rallies in droves. But the three friends soon forgot all about their personal experience until six months later, when a newspaper article caught Tina's observant eye.

> Well-known and respected evangelist minister Pastor Dennis remanded in connection with smuggling of contraband comprising gold watches and electronic goods worth one million US dollars…

'Didn't I tell you, that man is as crooked as they come?' remarked Rita jubilantly. 'Once a thief, always a thief!'

Manel was bitterly disappointed and insisted that there was possibly a misrepresentation of facts. The charismatic Dennis with his hypnotic eyes had very much swayed her. The girls followed the case with interest, but eventually, the news seemed to fizzle out. Dennis, no doubt, had the right connections to bail him out. The incident had a negative impact on his congregation. This was bad news; they began to doubt him.

But Dennis insisted on carrying on with the ministry, preaching, and confessing to his weaknesses of falling prey to evil. Yes, he had faltered, but he had repented of his sinful ways, and prayed fervently for God's forgiveness. And God had forgiven him… Hallelujah! Dennis re-established his former glory and ministered on.

*

Almost a year passed by and this time it was Manel who saw the news article, which made headlines.

Pastor Dennis Perera, well-known evangelist and faith healer, caught by customs inspectors in connection with the smuggling of illegal and harmful drugs worth ten million US dollars. Pastor Perera has been denied bail because of to the severity of the offence and several past convictions…

Manel, Tina, and Rita had a field day that evening, staying on into the late hours at Patti's Tea House.

The case dragged on for months and this time there was no wriggle room for His Holiness, the pastor. He received a ten-year jail term; and thus ended what could have been a lifelong career of hoodwinking a gullible congregation. Dennis Perera became a forgotten name within a few years.

*

Five years later at Welikada maximum security prison, the prison warden knocked on the door and waited.

'Come in.'

'Your Holiness…Pastor Dennis, they have asked me to summon you to a meeting with the superintendent. If you would just follow me, please… I'll escort you to his office.'

'Thank you, Sunil. You are a good man and God will surely bless you and your family,' said Pastor Dennis, giving Sunil a gentle pat on his shoulder.

'Thank you, Your Holiness. I feel most blessed to be addressed in such a manner by Your Holiness.'

They walked down and around a few corridors. The warden knocked on the superintendent's door and bowed as he ushered Pastor Dennis in. He closed the door, still bowing to Pastor Dennis. He was a reformed man since he had attended Pastor Dennis's prayer meetings.

'Ah! Here we are at last. Do sit down, Pastor Dennis,' said the superintendent. 'I hope your quarters are a little more comfortable since we last met. I asked the wardens to ensure that you have everything you need…within reason, of course.'

'I have no complaints, Brother John,' said Dennis. 'What I do hope is that you have some good news for me.'

'Of course, that is why I wished to see you,' said John in a semi-whisper. 'The seagull has landed, and it's roosting safely in its nest... awaiting further orders. Rather a big catch, I believe!'

'That's splendid news, John. In that case, we should celebrate... Any champagne?'

'At your service, Pastor Dennis,' remarked the superintendent as he deftly pulled out a bottle and two glasses from his drawer.

'The commissioner knows the situation then?'

'Of course. All's in order. Not a thing for you to worry about, sir,' remarked John. He was intoxicated with the thought of his cut, his dream life come true at last.

'In that case, I'll be sleeping well tonight.' Dennis smiled to himself. He would soon be a multimillionaire, jetting off into the sunset.

A Prickly Situation

Andy had just returned from a stressful day at work. He got off at Kilburn tube station and walked over to the off-licence to get himself a six-pack for the evening. This would be dinner tonight; he was in no mood to cook. Not only had he had some difficult customers to deal with that day, but returning home had proved to be a nightmare; football fans creating no end of racket, crowding the tube stations, and causing delay upon delay. He perked up as he approached home. His was a flat on the first floor of a 1930s-style house in a quiet residential street; he liked it there and had been there for almost four years, since 1970. That's when his short-lived marriage had broken up.

But parked next door was a removal van, and Andy certainly wanted to know who was moving in or out. As it turned out, someone was moving into the flat in the adjoining house. The flat was positioned right across from Andy's and had remained vacant for some time. He was close enough to see them now. Wow! he thought, she is a stunner. I hope that's not the boyfriend helping her. Time would tell, but for now, Andy had his eye firmly fixed on the girl as she lifted a box out of the van and lugged it inside. She had blonde hair which appeared to be tied up in a bun of sorts and the most fabulous Marilyn Monroe-like figure; her hips swayed as she moved. This was certainly enough to get Andy excited about his new neighbour. He bounded upstairs, humming a tune, and headed straight into the kitchen. From there, he had a bird's eye view of the neighbouring flat's sitting room.

The easy chair in the corner of Andy's kitchen provided an excellent vantage point for observing his new neighbour. Quickly he deduced that the bloke was merely a removalist; he appeared to obey orders on where to place the various boxes and, once all was done, he drove off in his minivan. That was a relief to Andy, who was already weighing up his opportunities with this beautiful addition to his street and possibly, very possibly, to his life. She certainly was a magnificent-looking creature, and now Andy had to get his action plan together. That evening passed too quickly and before he'd finished his last beer, the lights went out next door, leaving him brooding about the new girl in his street.

Daylight streamed in through the kitchen window. Andy realised he'd fallen asleep in his chair, and it was already time to get ready for work. He ached from the poor posture, but last night's excitement cheered him up as he washed and readied himself with a whistle and a hum. He kept popping into the kitchen to see if there was any activity in the flat next door, but all was quiet. Perhaps she was still asleep!

It was a cheerful Andy at work that morning. Andy always dressed well and today he had on one of his better suits, one with an Italian cut. It certainly put an edge to his tall, lean figure, which, despite the five decades spent, was in good shape. There were no grey hairs on his head and he looked years younger than he was.

'Got a new neighbour,' he said to his colleagues.

'Anyone interesting?' asked Colin.

'Interesting is not the word, Colin. She's bloody sexy. And what a figure! Can't wait to ask her out.'

'So, you'll be busy tonight then?' said Colin, with a knowing look at the others.

Everyone knew of Andy's many exploits with the opposite sex and looked forward to a saga of events that would inevitably come to an explosive end.

Andy sang and whistled all that day. During his lunch hour, he nipped down to the telephone box, not wanting others in the office to overhear him. He called his cousin Doug to share the news. He and Dougie were as thick as thieves and had shared many an adventure over the years. Doug was a few years older than Andy, thickset around the shoulders and of sturdy build. He was always genial and good company, highly sought after by the young girls in his office and around his neighbourhood. Doug revelled in all the attention he received and would often be out dancing into the early hours of the morning, unsurprisingly with a young chick.

'Dougie, it's Andy. How's life treating you, mate?'

'Good to hear from you, mate. Nothing much from my end, but I'm sure you're up to something,' said Doug, giving Andy the prompt that he was waiting for.

Andy soon expanded on the past evening's happenings.

'How about a drink tonight? We haven't caught up for weeks,' said Doug.

Andy hesitated. 'Er, perhaps not tonight. What about Thursday night? That way, I'll have more to say to you about progress over here,' replied Andy, trying to make it sound very important.

'Yes, righty-oh, let's meet on Thursday, usual place then,' said Doug.

Fate could not have been kinder to Andy that evening. He approached the exit of Kilburn tube station and found himself behind a familiar-looking, shapely figure. She was a few steps ahead of him. He recognised the swing of those hips. He kept pace behind her, wondering how best to approach her, finally deciding that it would be best to speak to her just outside her house, the semi-detached next to his.

'Oh, you live right next door to me,' said Andy, pretending surprise. 'Are you new to the area? I've not seen you around before.'

She turned round and smiled. 'I've only just moved in…just yesterday, in fact,' she replied. 'And yes, I'm very new to this area. I'm Julie,' she said, extending her hand in greeting.

'I'm Andy. How very nice to meet you,' replied Andy, taking hold of her hand in what seemed to be an eternal handshake.

Julie literally had to yank her hand away in the end.

'I've lived around here for God knows how long. I could show you around a bit. How about a drink sometime? Tonight perhaps?'

'That sounds lovely, Andy, but I'm working tonight. Saturday would be great if that suits you.'

'Sure, sure, Saturday would be fantastic. I'll come and collect you around six-thirty and we'll walk down to the local. How does that sound?'

'Superb,' replied Julie, tantalising Andy once again with her ravishing smile.

Minutes later, Andy was still standing outside, not believing his luck. 'I wonder what she does?' he thought. Certainly not office work to be working in the evenings. What did it matter, anyway? He could ask her all those questions on Saturday.

Dougie arrived just before six on Thursday evening, a bottle of whisky tucked under his arm. The two cousins embraced each other in greeting and embarked on their drinking spree in the sitting room. Occasionally they looked across the kitchen window, hoping to catch a glimpse of a beguiling figure; their efforts yielded no positive result. The lights were out. Perhaps she was at work. Once all the booze in the flat was consumed, they got their jackets on and strode off to the local.

After much revelry, the two cousins swaggered back homewards, arm in arm and airing a boisterous song with lines all mixed up.

'Blimey, Andy, look! Look at those plums on your neighbour's tree. I wouldn't mind a few of those right now. Here, let me give you a lift up.'

Doug had already lifted the nimbler Andy by his rear end and hoisted him on his shoulder before Andy could so much as protest. This was no simple task for two men in their mid-fifties. The property, which was two doors away from Andy's, belonged to an elderly, cantankerous man who rarely had a pleasant word for any of his neighbours. Andy had in the past had a few run-ins with him, and here he was now, frantically trying to grasp at the branches of the man's plum tree. Well, he was in the thick of it now. Best to make it as quick as possible. Andy was dangling, hanging precariously onto a branch, seemingly going nowhere.

'Swing yourself, old chap, get up there and fill your pockets,' said Doug. 'Here, let me give you a bit of help.' Doug took hold of both of Andy's dangling legs and swung them so that Andy could get them both around the branch.

Well, that made things slightly easier. Andy hooked his arm around a second branch and hoisted himself up so that he could stand with a leg on each branch. As he started picking the fruit, he heard a sound, one that was very familiar to his childhood. It was that creaking, give-way sound, which meant that his weight was too much for the branch to bear. He could see disaster unfolding, as it very predictably did.

The branch gave way and, as Andy's legs splayed, he wasn't sure if he heard his Savile Row trousers rip or whether it was just the wind escaping his digestive tract. It was a long and protracted whine. He hoped desperately that it was the latter, but sadly it was both. Andy clung to whatever he could, but as fate would have it, there was only one escape route. He came crashing down on his back with a thud, clinging onto the branches of a fine and prized variety of European sugar plum. While the fall was not that significant, the scream that emanated from Andy was blood-curdling. He had fallen on another of his neighbour's prized botanical specimens, a pincushion cactus of extraordinary size. The pain seared through the soft tissue of his rear end and knocked him unconscious. Andy's scream attracted quite a few of the residents, who rushed to the spot; among them was the property owner, the ill-tempered old man, who in panic was shouting all manner of abuse at Doug and the unconscious Andy. The two men were in the spotlight, with a multitude of torches flashing around them.

Julie had just left the house on her way to work but had stopped on seeing two shadowy figures behaving oddly next door. She rushed to the scene on witnessing the fall of a largish-looking object from the tree; it was when she shone her torch to see what had happened that she recognised the victim. Doug was relieved to see the uniform she wore; he heaved a sigh. What could be better than a nurse at hand, at a time like this! Julie realised the extent of the injury and immediately asked a passer-by to call the ambulance.

The thorns on the cactus were near-lethal and the ambulance workers had to take Andy with the cactus still stuck to his rear end to hospital. He was face down on the trolley. Julie got in the ambulance with him; it was much quicker getting to work this way. Besides, she knew the ambulance workers. Slowly but surely, they prised the cactus off, but there were so many thorns still stuck deep in Andy's flesh.

The tedious work of de-thorning Andy began in the emergency ward, and that is where Andy regained consciousness. The pain was indescribable, and he moaned repeatedly, not knowing what had hit him.

'You're all right, Andy, you're in expert hands,' said Julie comfortingly. 'You'll be as right as rain tomorrow.'

'Tomorrow? Tomorrow? What about right now? I'm in unbelievable agony,' wailed Andy. He paused a moment to think. 'Do I know you?' he questioned. 'Your voice sounds rather familiar.'

Julie knelt down in front of Andy. 'It's me, your new neighbour, Andy.'

'You're a nurse? I can't believe it. Oh no, you saw me fall off that tree and all!'

'Yes,' said Julie, with a smile on her face. 'I must admit it was all rather funny, especially that trumpet of wind as your trousers split.'

'Oh, damn, damn, damn! Why do I get into trouble every time I'm with Dougie? He's the one who made me do it. I'm not always like this, Julie,' wailed Andy with pleading eyes.

'I'm going to sedate you now, Andy, so you can…'

That was the last Andy heard as he slipped into peaceful oblivion.

Two weeks later, still limping with pain, Andy made his first appearance at work to a host of questions from his colleagues. They already had some interesting versions of his escapade. It was a difficult day, and he made his way home a bit earlier than usual; sitting was still rather awkward. As he approached home, he was suddenly aware of his hysterical neighbour, yelling and wielding a cricket bat at him.

'You hooligan! look at what you did to my beautiful garden…!'

Andy turned white as paper. Quick action was needed. He turned around and ran as fast as his aching rear and limp would allow. He would simply have to call Julie and ask her to make her own way to the pub for their first proper rendezvous.

The Silk Scarf

Nancy was keenly aware of being watched. Her eyes wandered to the front of the shop, then across the road to the row of shops on the other side. Her gaze moved slowly from right to left and back again; each time, it wavered in the centre. It was there in the centre, from across the road; she knew with certainty that she was being watched. A sudden chill made its way up her spine. This was the third day in a row that she had felt this discomfort; now she knew that it was not just her imagination. For amidst the throng of shoppers that jostled this way and that, one figure seemed to remain static, craftily mimicking the actions of a shopper but never quite moving away. His gaze met hers but quickly turned away; it gave her no more than a fleeting glimpse of his face. She saw him hastily purchase something from the street vendor before disappearing discreetly into the crowd. His face remained turned away from her at all times.

Having her suspicions confirmed perturbed Nancy. It was not yet closing time, but her instincts made her pull the shutters down on the shop window. Nancy had owned her little clothing store in Myanmar for almost thirty years. After many years of territorial unrest, she had moved to a little village about fifty kilometres south of Maung La, not far from the Chinese border. This was the first time she was closing her shop early. Ordinarily, there was good money to be made over the next couple of hours, but suddenly it all felt inconsequential. What was she going to do with all the money she had made, anyway? She had no child to leave it to; it was something she did not like to dwell upon but did quite frequently. How she longed to have had a child with the man she still loved so intensely. Slowly but surely, her mind made that journey back to her childhood days, to the time when she had first set eyes on her one true love.

Nancy turned off the lights in the shop and slowly made her way up the stairs to the little flat above the shop, her home. There she was at peace to reminisce, undisturbed by customers.

*

Tam Buk was the little village on the eastern border of Myanmar where Nancy, or Nan Ting as her parents had named her, had spent her childhood. She was the youngest of five. She knew little about the three older siblings; they had left the village and visited infrequently. It was just her youngest brother who worked with her father, her mother and herself left in the village. Money was scarce, and the burden of cooking and keeping house was already upon her since the tender age of twelve.

'Nan Ting, I feel unwell today. You will need to go down to the well for water. We'll need three buckets. When you have done that, I'll give you some money to go to the market... We need some fish and vegetables,' said her mother in a feeble voice.

'Yes, mother, shall I go now for the water?' questioned Nan Ting, with a sigh. She hated pulling water from the well. It was hard work, both dragging it out of the well, and then carrying it home, but there was little choice in the matter.

The well was communal, shared by a tiny and dwindling community that comprised the village. It was always busy as everyone needed water and often one had to wait for one's turn. The women did not seem to mind it; there was always lots of highly desirable gossip to exchange. But Nan Ting was not interested in what the women said. She simply wanted this chore to be over. The well was always a blaze of colour from the brilliant hued sarongs the women wore, but today Nan Ting saw something unusual. There were two male figures attired in Khaki outfits. 'That's what soldiers wear,' thought Nan Ting as she got closer. Her surprise doubled when one of the young men waved at her with a broad grin on his face.

'Nan Ting, it's me, Shin Tae. Have you forgotten me, my dear little cousin?'

Nan Ting's face broke into a jubilant smile. She dropped her bucket and ran up towards her cousin. He picked her up, and they hugged and clung to each other.

It must have been at least three years since she had last seen Shin Tae. He had left the village to look for work and, by the looks of it, had joined the army. All the while that Shin Tae twirled her around in the air, her eyes lay fixed on her cousin's companion. It was rare to see a white person, a European, in these parts of Myanmar. The newcomer completely tantalised Nan Ting. His tall stature, glowing white complexion, eyes as deep as the deep blue sea, and the most beautiful golden blond hair cropped short at the back, made him the most handsome man that she had ever set eyes on. Her hitherto dormant sexuality suddenly came alive, burning within her, rousing her desires to cherish this piece of perfection for eternity.

Suddenly her feet returned to the earth. She was dizzy, but more so from the sight of the newcomer than her cousin's twirling.

'Nan Ting, this is my good friend, Simon. He'll be staying a couple of days with me. Say hello to him,' urged Shin Tae, noticing Nan Ting's extremely red face and attributing it to shyness.

She managed a monosyllabic greeting and shook the outstretched hand, her first handshake and one that she was not going to forget.

'Hello, Nan Ting,' said Simon. 'I've heard a lot about you from your cousin,' said Simon, speaking Burmese with a strange accent that she found terribly exciting.

She smiled coyly at him and at that moment it felt as though that was all she could do; funny, she thought, how her tongue seemed tied, unable to say anything.

Thankfully, Shin Tae had lots of questions to divert her mind. 'How is your mother, Nan Ting? I heard the women here talk about her being ill. Is that so?'

'Yes, brother Shin,' said Nan Ting, addressing her cousin politely. 'She has not been well at all but we don't know what's wrong with her. Father says that we may have to take her to see a special doctor in the next village, but Mother does not want to go. It's hard for me, as I have to clean the house and do the cooking now,' said Nan Ting, ponderously surveying the bucket in her hand.

'That must be hard for a little girl like you,' remarked Simon. 'Come, Shin, let's help your cousin to get this water up to her house.'

Simon grabbed the pail from Nan Ting, filled it at the well, and the three of them walked up the footpath leading to Nan Ting's house. Nan Ting was glowing softly inside. She felt honoured that a European man was actually assisting her; in her village, a man rarely helped a woman to do what they regarded as women's work.

As they walked up to the house, she asked him how he had learned to speak her language. Simon told her that he had lived nearby for almost five years, as his father was doing some work for the Burmese government. He had always played with the local children and learnt the language with great ease.

Over the next few days, Shin Tae and Simon spent most of their time with Nan Ting; they helped her with getting water from the well, chopping firewood, and even cooking. Nan Ting was amazed that Simon did not mind doing all these female chores; she adored him for that very reason.

One day when they were at the well, he said that he was going to christen her.

'What does that mean, Simon?'

'It's how Christians name their children,' explained Simon. 'I'm going to pour some water on your head, and then I'm going to give you a new name that I have chosen for you,' remarked Simon.

They had both laughed at this.

Then, before she knew what was happening, Simon had poured a bucket of water on her head, and while she was squealing with both cold and delight, Simon made a cross on her forehead and said, 'I now baptise you and give you the name of Nancy.'

And that is how Nan Ting came to be known as Nancy. Nevermore thereafter did she refer to herself as Nan Ting. Nancy would never forget that moment; she felt forever bonded to Simon.

A terrible sadness overwhelmed her when soon after this, her cousin Shin Tae and Simon left. Their military leave was over and they would head towards the north-eastern border to maintain security. Nancy had bade them goodbye the previous evening, as their departure was scheduled for dawn the next day. She cried all night until dry tears smeared her face. Unbeknown to her mother or father, Nancy was up early the next morning to see two faint khaki-clad figures disappear into the distance. At dawn, she had opened the front door and stepped quietly into the comfort of the cool night air. As the two figures faded out of sight, she realised that life would simply resume its monotonous cycle; she had best get some sleep before it was too late. On entering the house, she noticed something dark on the doorstep; it was a small brown paper package tied up with ribbon. Upon it was something soft and fragrant, a magnolia, a smell she knew well. Nancy took the package into her tiny room and hid it under her bed. It was too dark to see as yet; she would wait until daylight allowed her to appreciate the contents. 'Thank you, Simon,' she whispered to herself.

What followed was one of the longest days in Nancy's memory. She had chores aplenty before attending school for the required minimum of three hours and then more housework on returning home at lunchtime. Concentrating on her lessons proved difficult that day. Her thoughts were on Simon, and she kept wondering what the package with the simple marking of 'to Nancy' contained. After lunch, her mother would lie down for her rest and Nancy would be at peace to do what she pleased. She had decided to take the package down to the river bank, to her special hideout within the confines of a large bush; this was her haven, away from prying eyes, and shaded from the midday sun.

Nancy had never known her heart to pound as it did then; there was no doubt in her mind that she loved Simon, and she was going to wait for his return for however long it took. She looked at the package, examining every feature before untying the delicate silk ribbon holding it together. Her little fingers were shaking with a mixture of anxiety and delight; never had she received a present in such a romantic fashion. Wanting this moment to last as long as possible, she held the package close to her cheek, seeking to seal the smell of its contents in her memory; the paper felt cool against her skin, and then she could wait no longer. She unwrapped the package carefully and gasped with delight as she unravelled a beautiful silk scarf. It had hues of deep blue and green mingled with pink. Nancy adorned herself with the scarf, first over her head, then over her shoulders and neck. This was the most beautiful piece of silk that Nancy had ever set eyes on. Soon she was daydreaming. She was with Simon, and they were holding hands and looking into each other's eyes. 'I will wait for you to return, Simon,' she said out loud.

*

It was time to open the shop once more. Nancy was ready to confront the stranger rather than keep battling with her fears. He was not there when she opened the blinds, but a couple of hours later, she noticed the now familiar figure. This time, his gaze was direct; their eyes met and, as if drawn by that gaze, he made his way across the road to her shop. Nancy's heart was racing, not knowing what to expect. The only comfort she had was the sturdy counter behind which she stood, wary and uncertain. He was there now, at the counter, a glimmer of a smile on his face.

'Nan Ting, do you not remember me, your cousin, Shin Tae?'

Nancy gasped and took a step back. She took in the now aged and battle-weary features. Yes, she could see the resemblance, even with the moustache that now adorned his creased face. Nancy's face broke out into a smile, and the tears streamed down her face as she stepped out from behind the counter to embrace her long-lost cousin.

'Shin Tae, this is almost too good to be true. I thought you were dead but here you are, alive and well, and how wonderful it is to see you after all these years.' She was sobbing uncontrollably as she hugged and held on to him, unable to say much more.

'I have searched for you for the past three years, Nan Ting Nancy.

26

All the villages along the border, one by one, and I had almost given up hope until I spotted you this week.'

'Come, come, we must talk and celebrate this reunion,' said Nancy. 'Let me close the shop and we can go upstairs and have some tea.'

Nancy was quick to close the shop down. She had no interest in business today. Today was for Shin Tae, dear Shin Tae. How she had missed him and thought of him all these years, never knowing what had happened to him or Simon when they left on that terrible day.

'Nancy, I did not mean to frighten you by staring at you during the last few days, but I did not know if you were married or what your situation was. I eventually asked a few of the shopkeepers nearby and they told me that you lived alone. Did you never marry, Nancy?'

'No, I never married.' Nancy beckoned Shin Tae to sit down and busied herself with making tea and getting some rice cakes out for refreshment.

They sat down together, curious about each other's past.

'And your parents, brothers, sisters?'

'All sadly dead, Shin Tae. I have been alone for many years now but finally managed to build up this business to make a living. I have been very fortunate in many ways. And you, Shin Tae? The last I saw you, many years ago, you and Simon went off to fight the rebel groups along the border. What happened to Simon?'

Shin Tae was all too aware of Nancy's feelings for Simon. He had suppressed his own feelings for her knowing that his future was uncertain, but now perhaps, there might be a chance, he thought. 'The fighting was quite bad at times, Nancy, but eventually, we managed to push back the rebels. There was a cost, of course. Many lives were lost, so I consider myself lucky to be alive. Simon was badly wounded in one of the attacks. His father had him flown back to England for treatment, so he was lucky, as well. Sadly, I have lost contact with him since but I imagine he is well and happy.'

Nancy took in all of this pensively. She realised she would never see Simon again. In her heart, she had known that all along, anyway. Hoping to meet up again was only a childhood dream, mere escapism. But she could take joy in being reunited with Shin Tae. This was indeed a dream come true.

Shin Tae sat up. His eye had caught sight of something. He walked over to the chair in the corner and took hold of the scarf draped over the back. 'You still have it,' cried Shin Tae with tears in his eyes. 'You still have it.'

It was a green and blue scarf. With a flash, Nancy realised that it was Shin Tae who had left her that scarf.

He brought it over to her and draped it across her shoulders. 'You look beautiful in it. I thought they were the best colours for you.'

'Yes, the colours are beautiful and now I must thank you for this beautiful gift, Shin Tae. I wear this almost all the time. Thank you so much for leaving such a beautiful present for me.'

How could she have made such a mistake, she thought. It was Shin Tae who cared for her. There was a need to rethink and take in both the past, and the present.

The next few weeks were the happiest that Nancy and Shin Tae had experienced in a long time. Slowly, they began to fill in the details of the intervening years, mostly the struggle to exist, to find those they once knew, and accept the joy that came with it. Shin Tae moved into the spare room and helped Nancy with the shop. They enjoyed each other's company and life began to feel beautiful. In the evenings, they would walk down to the river and watch the ducks and birds. Nancy was doing things she had never done before, and it was on one of those walks that Shin Tae asked her to marry him. She could not have asked for more.

The Excursion

It was ten o'clock, the appointed time for gathering in the East Dell. Six of the eight biology majors had arrived. Ms Elizabeth Trent looked anxiously at her watch. As head of the biology department, she ran a tight ship and was formidable as a leader. Her physical appearance and demeanour were daunting. Almost six feet in height, her large and cumbersome body frame with that unconcealable stoop showed the distinct signs of ageing. Her body leaned towards the left, showing wear and tear of either hips or knees. Yet, despite this physical degeneration, nothing sullied Ms Trent's spirits. Hers was a determination that nothing could dampen, and she demanded of her students, a total dedication to the study of the fauna and flora, no ifs or buts. Many a girl would tremble in front of her, forget what they meant to say or ask, often saying yes when they meant no and vice versa. We were third-year biology majors.

Trent's second-in-charge was the newly arrived Ms Dixon, emeritus professor of biology. With a relaxed and cheerful personality, Ms Dixon had a calming effect on Ms Trent. The two had known each other for close to forty years. Ms Dixon, though older, appeared far better preserved physically than her associate. She had a shock of white hair and an eternal smile adorned her face. She always had something cheerful to say. We assumed she had only trekked half the globe in her lifetime as opposed to Trent, who seemed to have done the entire planet several times over. Trent had a burning thirst for knowledge that seemed unquenchable; she deserved every bit and more of the position she held at this prestigious women's college, situated in the foothills of the Blue Ridge Mountains of Virginia.

'I do believe I can see two young ladies making their way towards us,' said Ms Dixon as she peered into the distance with a pair of binoculars. 'Yes, that's Penny and Deanne making their way. Isn't this absolutely fabulous? We have a gorgeous day for our excursion, and Liz, I do believe you'll be seeing all those wonderful mushroom species that you wish to point out to the girls.' Trent was a dedicated botanist while Dixon had specialised in palaeontology.

'Sorry, Ms Trent, sorry, Ms Dixon,' said the two girls, slightly out of breath from running down the hill.

'Good morning to you ladies,' said Ms Trent and nodded from side to side; it was a behaviour common to her and showed her general approval and pleasure. She surveyed all of us, her smile indicating her genial mood. The excursions into the woods meant a lot to her, and she and Dixon had prepared a large hamper of food for our picnic lunch to follow.

'Well, I must say that we are fortunate to have such a glorious day! Fine weather as well. And it's the perfect season for us to see some of the plant and animal life that we'll be studying this semester. There's absolutely nothing that competes with seeing the fauna and flora in their natural habitats,' said Trent, looking down towards her left breast and adjusting the bluebells that she had pinned to her dress. 'The West Dell behind the refectory has an abundance of these. Such a magnificent sight! Make sure you get a glimpse of them before they wither away, young ladies...and consider yourselves very lucky indeed to be in such a privileged place as this, hm... Well, Ms Dixon and I also have a little surprise for you.' She nodded at Dixon with a twinkle in her eye. 'But we'll tell you all about that during our lunch...and we hope that you'll be just as excited about it as we are. I believe we are ready to get started? Make sure you stick to the trail...we don't wish to destroy what nature has given us.'

Trent led the group towards a track, taking them into the woods beyond the dell. Her greying hair was done up in a bun, giving full exposure to the bright blue flowers she had stuck in her ears. She was a true-blue botanist indeed!

'Lucy, stay on the path. That's what it's there for.'

'Yes, Ms Trent. Sorry, Ms Trent,' said Lucy

'Jessie, you've just put your foot down on a crocus.'

'Sorry, Ms Trent,' replied Jessie as she stifled a laugh and wondered what a crocus looked like. She prodded Claire, who was next to her, and said, 'Your turn next, I think.'

'I heard that,' remarked Ms Trent, 'Hm…and as we now know who's next in line… Claire, are you able to tell us which bird is singing that beautiful song?'

'Deanne, you really must tone down that voice of yours. It's disturbing our nocturnal friends.'

'Yes, Ms Trent,' replied Deanne in an even louder voice than before.

Somewhere in the middle of the group, Ms Dixon was heard chuckling to herself. 'Liz, you haven't changed one iota in all the years I've known you. And girls, if you must know, it's quite a few decades that Ms Trent and I have worked together.'

We were quite accustomed to the ways of Ms Trent, this being our third year with her. She still came across as an awe-inspiring individual that none of us would wish to cross. After all, who knew what we might evoke in her in terms of retribution? One thing that she certainly made most of us feel was that our knowledge of biology was deeply lacking. It was perhaps her reason for spending so much of her free time organising social-cum-study sessions such as this to lift us up to an acceptable level. We all appreciated the social aspect, as this was a residential college. We were all away from home and our families. To have Ms Dixon along on this particular occasion was indeed a bonus. She was such a contrast to Trent and helped to lighten the atmosphere. We thought of her as belonging to the student cohort as opposed to being part of the teaching team. Her presence during our third year of study would make a world of difference to our biology classes.

The excursion certainly invigorated and intrigued us. Several plant and animal species were spotted and identified. We made brief notes in the notebooks that we carried on all our biological outings; we would refer to them as and when we encountered the species during our study programme.

Of course, it was the picnic that was of utmost importance, now that we had finished the official business. We were back at the point where we had started and found a cool spot under some trees to lay out our spread. It was time to consume some of the treasured plant species we had encountered in some form or other: dandelion salad, stinging nettle and chickweed sandwiches, garlic mustard spread, fried mushrooms, pine needle tea, and much more. It opened up a new world of food to us, both exciting and disgusting to our taste buds at the same time. I believe we never appreciated the time that our instructors invested in our well-being; this feast that they had prepared would have taken a few days to get together. We were replete and now it was time for that big surprise.

Ms Trent readjusted her position to gain our attention. 'Well, ladies…it's time for the big news that I promised you. Ms Dixon and I have been most fortunate to organise something rather special for you… a three-day excursion to the Smithsonian in Washington DC for us all. Does that excite you?'

Of course, all our faces lit up.

'That sounds awesome,' chimed a few of us.

'When are we going?'

'How will we be travelling to DC?'

We had so many questions, but Ms Trent had more to say about the excursion itself.

'What's special about this trip is that we have been granted permission to visit the underbelly of this esteemed organisation through Ms Dixon's extensive network of contacts. We will have access to the workrooms of the palaeontology department along with a guide who will explain to us how the specimens are cleaned, prepared and stored before going out on exhibit. Isn't that absolutely marvellous? I believe there will be few lectures on the origin and evolution of the species thrown in as well. Is that right, Jane?'

We were awestruck. This was going to be one hell of an exciting adventure, especially as Ms Dixon would accompany us. She was so good at breaking the monotony of Ms Trent's curt remarks. Ms Dixon was teaching us a course on evolution this semester and the trip was going to be the highlight of her course.

We set off on a Tuesday morning. Four travelled in Ms Trent's car and four in Ms Dixon's. The two-hour drive ended in a motel where shared rooms had been booked for us. After a quick lunch, we had a two-hour ride around Capitol Hill and its surrounds. For many of us, it was our first visit to the capital.

Later, and without our instructors, we toured the locality by foot to familiarise ourselves with what was around us. Penny was the first to alert us to a bottle shop close to us. Our minds were thinking in unison. It was a pleasant evening followed by dinner at a famous Chinese restaurant, again to expose us to a variety of foods that normally would not feature as part of our diet. Our appointment at the Smithsonian was at ten o'clock the next morning.

Dr Davis addressed us. He was going to be our guide for the day and the next morning. He was also Ms Dixon's brother-in-law and our all-important permit to enter high-security places within the museum complex. We felt most indebted to him and Ms Dixon for affording us this magnificent opportunity; it was very much a once-in-a-lifetime event.

Dr Davis gave us a brief talk before walking us through the public exhibition areas of the dinosaur collection with a running commentary. Plant evolution was by no means overlooked. We saw many forms of fossilised plant life preserved in a variety of forms over several millennia. Ms Trent was enthralled. She urged us to make notes on several of the species that we would later encounter in our studies. Lunch followed and then came the exciting part. We were escorted into the dungeons of the Smithsonian, where scientists from many fields of study moved silently in their white gowns. Our chatter soon died into whispers in acknowledgement of the general mood.

The storage spaces had to be commensurate with the size of the specimens being worked on, some huge, others much smaller, and some even minuscule. We were first taken into one of the larger rooms, where a dinosaur found on the African continent was being assembled, bit by bit. There were props to hold the main body frame until supporting limb bones could be attached. We watched fascinated as we saw how bones were cast to create permanent templates so that work could begin on recreating lost parts. They kept the environment as sterile as possible. Temperatures were controlled to reduce attack by microorganisms and general decomposition. From our point of view, it was all mind-boggling, a scenario we had not expected or thought of, given the size of some specimens. It was a massive amount of information to take in that day, yet unbelievably enlightening. That visit certainly defined career paths for some of us in later life.

It was almost six in the evening when we finished that Wednesday. Our two instructors had planned on a famous Sicilian restaurant for dinner. That was yet another experience. We watched the chefs making the dough for the pizza bases, expertly flinging it in the air several times until it was thin, light and as large as an oversized dinner plate. This was the evening that we all bonded. Instructors and students were both completely relaxed as we talked about what we had seen and learned that day. Ms Trent had a small quiz prepared for us and the one with the most points won a prize: a box of chocolates. It went to Jessie, the most serious of us students. Well exhausted by the end of that day, we were more than happy to retire to bed, but how could we let this opportunity go by so easily? This was going to be our last night in DC!

Penny and Deanne volunteered to go to the bottle shop while the rest of us changed into our nightwear and congregated in their room. The quantity of alcohol they brought back was mind-blowing, enough to last us a week! There were shrieks of excitement amidst concerns. Should we really drink so much? What of tomorrow? Would we be up to the task by morning? Somehow, the excuses against consuming all the booze became weaker by the minute.

'Well, there's something for everyone here. We've got beer, vodka, gin, rum and bourbon, so help yourselves. Who's for beer, for starters?' queried Deanne.

As most hands went up for the beer, we decided on starting with that and then moving on to the harder stuff. Penny and Deanne passed the cans around. As far as the drinks were concerned, the two girls proved themselves to be real pros. They had not forgotten the mixers; soda, tonic, tomato juice, orange juice and tabasco were all there to hand. The toilet mugs were soon put to more sociable uses as we tried the various mixes, some appealing, others not. After about an hour, the noise had risen to a crescendo and then decreased as intoxication took hold of us one by one. Jessie and Carrie fell asleep on the floor and remained there until the next morning. The rest of us dragged ourselves in semi-stupor to our rooms, leaving Deanne, Penny, and Tilly happily finishing what was left.

When the wake-up alarms went off the next morning, we were none too happy to get up, or consider the questions we should ask during the final wind-up of our tour. Tired and still intoxicated, we made our way to the meeting point for an early breakfast, and there put on brave faces for Trent and Dixon. Then, feigning enthusiasm, we fronted up to our guide, Dr Davis. Had any of us so much as formulated any questions about the exhibits of the previous day? No, was the categoric answer. So we were utterly relieved when Vera, being in a better state than the rest of us, carried the show for all of us.

'Dr Davis, you mentioned that the first winged dinosaurs were an absolute failure because of the lack of feathers. You indicated that they had skin similar to that of modern-day bats. Does that mean that bats are low down on the evolutionary scale? Like a living relic of the past, perhaps?'

'That's an excellent question, Vera…' Dr Davis's voice trailed off into the late Jurassic period without us, his audience.

We had more urgent business to attend to. Claire looked out of sorts, turned paper-white and crumpled in a heap at our feet. She was as cold as ice on a mountain slope. We drew back aghast with shock, then quickly laid her out on her back and undid her tightly buttoned-up shirt. Trent and Dixon speedily moved us away from her and fanned her until her eyes fluttered. Carrie was quick to provide the commentary.

'Oh! Ms Trent, Claire has not been feeling well these last few days. She was almost wanting to opt out of this trip but we convinced her that she must come. Perhaps a bit of quiet will help her recover. Shall we take her over to the cafeteria?'

In all honesty, we all felt that we could have done with either fainting or puking after the night's alcohol feast. In our naivety, we thought that we had pulled the wool over our tutors' eyes; they, of course, knew better! The session ended earlier than planned, and soon after lunch, we were on our way back to college.

Carrie insisted on sitting next to Claire; she was in overdrive, trying to convince Ms Trent of Claire's ill health. 'Do you know, Ms Trent, that Claire suffers from mononucleosis. She only told us about it a few weeks ago when we asked her why she doesn't take part in a lot of things. These couple of days have been too much for her system to cope with. It's probably why she passed out…'

Carrie was in excellent form, exercising her verbosity to the point of becoming tiresome to the rest of us, travelling in Ms Trent's car. Her tenacity towards convincing Ms Trent that this incident was entirely a result of Claire's poor health was unbearable. All of us of course, had had an early night in preparation for the final day, claimed Carrie. She was so relentless in trying to convince Ms Trent of this untruth that it eventually lulled us off to sleep. Perhaps she did convince Ms Trent in the end, but Ms Trent was intent on having the last say in the matter.

We arrived on campus and, to our shock, found that the first stop was at the infirmary where Claire was to spend the night before being examined by the campus doctor the next morning. We gaped in disbelief while Claire simply glared at us, outraged at her fate. But the matter was settled; there was nothing we could do to reverse Ms Trent's decision.

We were well sober and repentant when we encountered our two formidable mentors the following week. There was much to write about in our notebooks – something we would wish to revisit in the future. Our visit to the Smithsonian with Ms Trent and Ms Dixon would remain a landmark event of our four years at college. The learning went much further than academia; it incorporated camaraderie, leadership, loyalty, power, and much, much more.

Epilogue – The Visit

Tiredness had overcome me. The trip down south from Washington DC was arduous. It was Carrie's incessant chatter; it had exhausted all of us. After Claire was placed in the competent hands of the nurse at the infirmary, the rest of us disembarked at the information centre. I lugged my overnight case across the quad and up the three flights of wooden stairs to my dormitory room. This was one of the older buildings on campus. It had no lift. It was also the mid-1970s, so there were no wheels on bags; with two large textbooks in my overnight case, I had a significant weight to carry. My roommate Dede was there to greet me, eager and all ears to hear what the trip had been like. Dede was very much the tomboy, always getting into one scrape or the other and often recruiting me as her accomplice; her stories amused the girls in our dorm to no end. Dede was dismayed to hear that Claire had to stay overnight in the infirmary; Dede and Claire were best friends.

'Sod it, poor Claire! I was really hoping to catch up with her over dinner. Come on, Sal. We've got half an hour. Let's see if we can have a quick visit with her.'

I changed into fresh clothes, and we headed out into the cool freshness of the evening. The hydrangeas around the infirmary were in bloom and a full moon was only just making itself visible, casting subtle shadows on the foliage. While this magnificent property hid a dark and hideous heritage of having been a slave plantation, today its role was without blemish, a place for the education and character development of young women and held in the highest esteem.

Our dormitory faced the rear of the infirmary, an old building of red brick. We walked around to the front door, which was approached by about ten steps. The lights were on downstairs. It was clear by the sign outside that visitors were not permitted at this time of the evening. Regardless, Dede kept knocking incessantly. We tried the door, but it was locked.

'Surely someone has to hear us!' she said.

'Perhaps the nurse has gone home.'

'She can't just leave when someone's in there. I think she's just pretending not to hear us.'

We kept knocking and shouting and ultimately gave up our quest for the night. There was always tomorrow, and Dede knew that she would have my support.

After breakfast, Dede and I made our way to the infirmary once again. There was no reason why we shouldn't be able to see Claire this time, and we expected her to be discharged that morning, in any case. The door was ajar, and we approached the nurse who sat at her desk, close to the entrance. How crisp she looked in that starched white uniform and white cap pinned to her hair.

The nurse looked up from her paperwork. 'Can I help you?'

'We've popped along to see how Claire is doing. Could we say hello to her?' questioned Dede.

'Claire is not well, and no, you most certainly can't see her.' The nurse was abrupt and sharp and felt no reason to provide us with an explanation. Yes, she was arrogant and had no time for the spoilt kids of this college that she worked at. Her attitude stood out a mile. She gave us an extremely disapproving look and beckoned us to the door with the simple movement of her chin in that general direction.

I shrank back in fear.

But Dede would not give up. 'If Claire is not well, we have a right to visit her. Your visiting hours are displayed on the door and we aren't violating them.'

'I'm afraid you can't visit her because she's got an infectious disease.'

'And what infectious disease is that?'

'Doctor has seen her this morning and diagnosed her with chickenpox.'

Dede was quick to change her tone. 'Please, can we see her for just a few minutes, just to say hello?'

'Under no circumstances! I will not have this entire campus come down with chickenpox... I will happily let her know that you came along...let me have your names then.'

Dede tried once more to plead with the nurse, only to receive a hostile 'Leave at once before I have you removed by the Pinkertons!'

As Dede and I turned reluctantly to leave, we saw the mail van drive up. It appeared as though the nurse was waiting in great anticipation for him to arrive. Her face broke out in a beaming smile. She bounced off her chair in such a rush that she knocked a pile of papers onto the floor. Not stopping to pick them up, she brushed past us, ran out of the door, and sprinted down the steps to get the mail. Both of us were left astounded at this extraordinary change of mood to her sour demeanour. We looked questioningly at each other, and then, with lightning speed, decided that this was our moment of opportunity. We ran in the opposite direction, up the stairs to the landing, where Claire was waiting anxiously for us. She was so glad to see both of us, as much as we were to see her. But what now?

Claire looked around quickly and then beckoned us to get into the walk-in closet. We expected the nurse to come upstairs any minute, so we conversed in hushed tones through the half-open closet. We heard the door downstairs bang shut. The nurse must be back. Claire tiptoed to the landing to look downstairs. She came back to report that the nurse was not at her desk; she was no doubt doing some other work downstairs. We felt more relaxed to come out of the closet, speak in less hushed tones.

'Nursy wouldn't let us come and visit you, saying you had the chickenpox. Is that so, Claire?'

'I'm afraid so. She's called my parents and they're coming over to pick me up tomorrow morning. I could stay here, of course, but Mum and Dad feel I'd be better off recuperating at home.'

'We're going to miss you, Claire. When do you get back?' I asked.

'Two weeks, I believe. I'm not quite sure, but that seems about right. We had a great time in DC, though, didn't we?' She smiled at me, recalling our little adventure at the Smithsonian. 'It sure was awesome. Apart from me fainting of course, which we thought was from the drinking…but as it turns out, I've got the pox.'

We laughed as we recollected the incident.

It was time to check on nursy again. Dede and I had classes at ten that morning and we had to find a way out without her seeing us. Claire tip-toed once again to the landing. Still no sign of nursy. We decided to spend a few more minutes with Claire before making a dash out of the infirmary. It was then that we heard faint cries from outside. The sash windows were down and muffled the exact nature, but it sounded like someone calling out for help. Claire went over to the corner of the window and took a peek through the curtains. Very quickly, she pulled herself back.

'It's nursy,' she said. 'She's outside, just beneath this room. Listen, there she goes again… Can you hear what she's saying?'

We were both straining hard to figure out what she was shouting about. What were we to do? If we left now, we'd walk straight into her on the drive. Perhaps she knew we were upstairs and was challenging us. I was panicking and so was Claire, but Dede was as bold as brass. And then, the strangest thing happened. Little stones kept bouncing off the windowpane. Ping, ping! The shower got louder and thicker by the second. Claire was panicking. She went up to the window and opened it.

'Help!' shouted nursy. 'I'm locked out. I need to get back in.'

On hearing the response, Dede and I dashed over to the window. All three of us hung our heads out defiantly.

'I'm locked out. Can you let me in, please?' Nursy had forgotten her arrogance. 'I came out to collect the mail, and the wind shut the door on me. I don't have my keys on me. Do you think you two could come down and let me in, please?'

All three of us clattered down the stairs and opened the door to let in an extremely flustered and red-faced nurse. She kept explaining that had she not forgotten her keys, she would not be in such a predicament.

'Well,' remarked Dede, 'what a good thing that we hung around in that case or you would have had to call the Pinkertons to let you in. Wouldn't that have been embarrassing?'

'Yes, girls, I'm so glad that you had not left…and thank you for letting me in. I'm sure Claire has enjoyed your visit… And you can stay longer if you wish to,' she added, noticing that we were about to depart.

'Thanks, nurse. We only wanted to say hello to Claire and wish her well. Anyway, we've got to get to class soon. Thanks for the visit. We might come by this evening, though.'

'That would certainly be fine…and thank you, girls.'

We bade farewell to Claire and ripped our sides out, laughing as we walked back to the dormitory.

The Elegant Mrs Melder and Her Grandson

It was Sunday; the streets of Colombo were quiet and even quieter out in the suburbs. It was in the suburbs that the mother church of the Anglican community occupied a beautifully elevated position overlooking the harbour. Built of stone in the traditional English style, its simple elegance commanded attention. Sadly, the membership was in free fall since the declaration of independence in 1948. The once overwhelmingly European congregation was leaving the island, and the demographics of both nation and church were changing. The church fellowship now comprised a small contingent of native Ceylonese mixed with a handful of bi-race European families. Regardless, the church remained the focal point of social interaction.

The Reverend Father Perera, the verger, and the altar boys made their way to the entrance of the church, marking the end of the morning service. The congregation followed, meandering out to greet the day. It was a radiant morning, and the splash of colour on the lawn against that beautiful tropical blue sky with its lofty white clouds was indeed a feast for the eye.

This was the first Sunday of the month and, as customary, was marked by a morning tea on the lawn overlooking the harbour. The church committee was already busy laying out tables for the cakes, biscuits, tea and soft drinks. As always, the sweeping branches of the flaming flamboyant, heavily laden with blossom, were nature's protection from both the odd shower and the tropical sun. Beneath that canopy of scarlet mingled the small gathering of colourfully dressed churchgoers and, against the grey backdrop of the church, the image was none other than stunning. Everyone looked forward to these social events to catch up on what was new. It was also the ideal occasion for getting into one's

Sunday best, very much the talking point amongst the ladies. Father Perera enjoyed the social aspect as well, regardless of his quiet and reserved nature. He was a keen observer of his congregation and listened intently to all around him.

Carrie had her eye on a cream cake and ran to join her friend Leslie, who seemed to be thinking along the same lines. They always had lots to catch up on as they did not attend the same school; besides, Carrie had not been to church for the past two Sundays. Her family were not regular churchgoers. Their attendance was patchy, but when it came to dressing up, Carrie's mother did it in style and spared nothing on herself or her eleven- and twelve-year-old daughters. They always looked picture-perfect.

'Carrie! Who made that beautiful dress for you? I wish I could have one like that,' said Leslie.

'Do you like it? It's my birthday dress.'

'My mum says that you and your sister have beautiful clothes, just like your mother. I think she envies your mother a lot,' remarked Leslie.

'I'm going to have one of these cream cakes,' said Carrie, taking a huge bite that left frothy white frosting all around her mouth. 'Mmm! That really tastes good.'

Leslie followed suit with a 'Yum' of appreciation. They had just started talking about things at school when they heard Carrie's mother.

'Carrie, Carrie, come over here, please.'

Carrie stuffed the rest of her cream cake in her mouth and skipped across to her mother's side.

'This is Mrs Melder. Say how do you do to her.'

'How do you do, Mrs Melder?' said Carrie, extending her hand.

'My dear girl,' said Mrs Melder, as she grasped Carrie's hand and kept hold of it. 'Do you know how much you look like me when I was your age? Why, I could have thought I was looking at myself.' She drew close to Carrie, as if wanting to hug her.

Mrs Melder was amazingly strong and fit for her age. She was slender and always dressed in expensive, high-quality imported clothes. The ladies envied her fabulous handbags and shoes, and just about everyone commented on her array of gorgeous hats. Hats were no longer in fashion, but Mrs Melder was very much old school and upheld her traditional European roots. She was grandmother to none other than Bernard Box, the annoying little urchin that all the girls hated.

'Did your mummy make that beautiful dress for you, darling? You look gorgeous in it. I love to dress up in nice clothes too, as you can see. You take care of yourself, darling, and I'll look forward to seeing you in church next Sunday,' she said, still holding Carrie's hand and stroking it with the other.

'Thank you, Mrs Melder. Goodbye, Mrs Melder,' remarked Carrie, looking rather pleased with the attention.

'Now, where's that grandson of mine? I have to get him back to his mother before he gets into any trouble. Bernard! Bernard!' she called out, looking around her. It was while she was looking around and calling for Bernard that the serenity of the moment was shattered and mayhem broke loose.

'Look out! Get away from the belfry.'

Someone had spotted something happening up in the tower; the warning shouts made some rush away, while others simply froze to the spot. The next moment, a shower of small stones and rocks came crashing down into the crowd. Soon everyone was scrambling away from under the belfry, having divested themselves of their cakes and cups of tea, which now lay scattered on the ground. In disbelief, eyes focused upward to the tower. To no one's surprise, the quirky, mischievous face of none other than Bernard Box peeked out of the small, slat-like window. He scowled before hurling the rest of his rock collection into a horrified crowd and an utterly mortified Mrs Melder.

The Reverend Father Perera was quick to run up the winding stairs to the belfry to apprehend the offender, whose location was thankfully devoid of an escape route. The stairs proved challenging in the long priestly garb but there was no urgency; Bernard had no way out. Father Perera dragged Bernard by the scruff of his neck down the narrow spiral stairway. They emerged to confront an audience that was curious to know how Father Perera would deal with the situation.

Bernard was fair-complexioned, much like his grandmother, and lanky. The ten-year-old had been spruced up in his Sunday by Mrs Melder. He wore a white shirt with short sleeves that now hung limply over his grey flannel shorts. His black shoes were scuffed and his grey knee-high socks, having heeded the force of gravity, lay crumpled at his ankles. There were gasps and whispers from the crowd, even unkind comments about the boy's unruliness. They fell silent as Father Perera marched Bernard straight into the vestry. There, he recived a sound talking-to and hiding.

Poor Mrs Melder, shaken by her grandson's behaviour, pleaded with tears in her eyes for compassion from Father Perera; there was good reason behind his behaviour, as she explained. Bernard came from a broken family. The separation of his parents had traumatised Bernard, and his consequent aggressive behaviour was turning the lives of his family members into a nightmare. This was later revealed to Carrie's mother by a distraught Mrs Melder.

The morning's events had certainly put a damper on the social gathering. Everyone pitched in to clean up the mess and pick up the stones that now littered the driveway to the church entrance and the stairs leading out to the road. The incident sparked a recollection of other events involving the infamous Bernard and his family, rumoured to be in serious financial trouble as well. This seemed rather intriguing to Father Perera, given the extravagant manner in which Mrs Melder dressed and it raised questions about how much of what was being said was outright gossip; there was plenty of that in circulation.

'Oh yes, people will lie through their teeth to make excuses for their children's behaviour,' said Mrs Hansen. 'Remember all the fibs that Geetha's parents told us, simply to hide their daughter's indiscretions. All Geetha needed was some strong discipline which she never got. Instead, they made up all manner of lies thinking they could fool us.'

'I remember Geetha,' piped in Mrs Abeyaratne. 'I totally agree with you, Mrs Hansen. There was absolutely no need for all those lies. Those parents of hers simply did not know how to control her. Thank God we're rid of that family.'

And so the tongues wagged. Today, however, those whose curiosity about the happenings in the vestry was greater than they could control found reason to linger, waiting for Mrs Melder and company to emerge from within.

Father Perera was more than exasperated after the event; not just with Bernard, but also with Bernard's grandmother. Being rather closed-minded, he was critical about the mothers and how they brought up their children; he rarely gave thought to all the work they put into raising funds for the church, or the immense responsibilities they coped with outside the church. Currently, his ears reverberated with Bernard's wails and Mrs Melder's pleas, and he was on the verge of accusing Mrs Melder of a particular indiscretion that had been bothering him for a while. He restrained himself. Two attacks on the same family on the one day were definitely too much. It could wait. At the moment, young Bernard was the primary concern, and after a good talking to with Bernard on his knees, Father Perera felt he had redeemed the situation for the moment. Bernard was dismissed and a lamenting and woeful Mrs Melder ushered him out. Father Perera was not one to endear himself to the younger generation; patience was not one of his virtues.

'Bernard! When I tell your mother about all this, she's going to make you kneel on a jackfruit* for two hours and I will be there to make sure you do it,' cried Mrs Melder to an unrepentant Bernard.

Next Sunday, Mrs Melder arrived without her grandson; everyone sighed with relief, most of all Father Perera. Nothing could be so perfect for him; he delivered his sermon without the disturbances usually caused by Bernard. He secretly hoped that he would never see Bernard again, and then quickly asked God for his forgiveness for being so selfish

* A large oblong green fruit found in tropical climates, measuring around sixty by thirty centimetres with a thick spiny hide. Kneeling on the jackfruit was often used as a punishment for children.

in his thoughts. With the service over and greetings having gone most cordially, Father Perera made his way to the vestry to count the day's takings. He was once again dismayed, and even more annoyed, to find dress buttons reappearing in the collection bag. He knew full well that they belonged to the well-heeled Mrs Melder.

Angry thoughts crowded Father Perera's mind, and he determined that there was no option but to confront Mrs Melder about this appalling situation. He knew with certainty that she was the culprit; over the past three or four months, he had diligently recorded his observations. The buttons did not appear when Mrs Melder did not attend church. It was time to take action.

Wednesday evening was Evensong and Mrs Melder arrived as usual, dressed in a bewitching outfit with hat, bag and shoes to match. The service ended and after the usual greetings, Father Perera quietly and deftly guided Mrs Melder into the vestry. He offered her a seat, which she took with a look of bewilderment. She had not brought Bernard along, so what could possibly be the matter? Father Perera then emptied the contents of the collection bag onto his desk. There among the coins and banknotes were three bright yellow buttons with gilt edging.

'Mrs Melder,' said Father Perera, picking up the three buttons and handing them to her, 'I believe these are yours. Aren't they?'

'Well, to be absolutely correct, they were mine, but now they belong to God. I gave them to God this evening. Don't you think they look beautiful?' She gazed longingly at them. 'They really brightened up my cream-coloured shirt... You know, the one with the lace around the neck. Unfortunately, I caught the sleeve on a nail that I hadn't noticed on my bedside table... I ended up tearing that beautiful shirt almost in two. My sister sent it to me...all the way from Australia, almost three years ago. In fact, she sends me all of my beautiful outfits.'

'Mrs Melder, what do you expect me to do with these buttons? Do you think that I can further the work of God when all you can put in the collection bag are buttons?'

Mrs Melder sat silent for a while and then began her explanation.

'Father Perera, I get the impression that you consider me to be well off because I am nicely dressed. Well, I'm afraid that is not the case. My sister and I were orphaned at a very young age...we were brought up in a convent but had no parents to help us along in later life. I married young and perhaps a bit unwisely. My husband drank and gambled away all his earnings...he died in his mid-thirties, leaving me with three children, one of whom was disabled. Caring for my three children led me down a spiral of poverty. It was only later in life that my sister, having done better than me, could help me out. It is still a meagre existence I lead, and the clothes she sends me are the only things that brighten my day. So, in answer to your question, I have no money to put in the collection bag and I am sure that God is happy with the beautiful buttons I give him. They are the best I have.'

Father Perera was shaken and humbled. After a brief silence, he cleared his throat and said, 'Mrs Melder, I am indeed very sorry to hear about your troubled life, and I beg you to forgive me for my rash demands on you. If there is anything that I can do to help you, please don't hesitate to ask. I have been a rather hard taskmaster, and your story has brought me down to earth. I must thank you for that... May I just ask, your daughter, Bernard's mother, is she suffering some financial difficulty since her marriage broke up?'

'Yes, I'm afraid she is. Her husband has run off with another woman and has left her high and dry with Bernard and his two younger sisters to care for. I do what I can for them, but in terms of money, I am very limited. It seems like her life reflects mine in many ways. I can only hope that there will soon be some light at the end of the tunnel for her.'

'Thank you for confiding this in me, Mrs Melder. Now that I know the circumstances, perhaps I might be the first person to provide a ray of light in your daughter's life. The church has funds to help the needy and I will submit your daughter's name for some financial assistance, if she approves, of course. I'll make a note and try and visit her tomorrow. It would be good if we can talk things over a bit. Will she be home around three in the afternoon? Perhaps you could come along as well?'

'Oh, that would be absolutely wonderful, Father Perera. Thank you so much for listening to me. Laura would be absolutely over the moon, and I'll make sure we are both there at three.'

Mrs Melder departed, leaving Father Perera in deep thought. The two people that he had despised most in his congregation had provided him with an epiphany. They had opened his eyes to the reality of life and stirred compassion in him, something he had not experienced before. He realised that he was only just beginning to understand the true nature of his vocation.

After the collection the following Sunday, Father Perera turned to the altar for the thanksgiving. '…we give thanks to thee, O God, and offer unto you these gifts of many and varied nature…'

Almost no one noticed the subtle change of wording apart from Mrs Melder.

A Marriage of Tribulation:
Fulham to Paris and Back

'Have you started already, you good for nothing English man? I wish you would die so I could get on with my life. Why do I have to clear up your mess all the time? Here, drink all you want!' Theresa tipped the wine bottle, pouring more on the table rather than in his glass.

She was livid with rage in that very expressive French way of hers. It was eight in the morning; she was getting ready for work. Theresa was the manageress of a high-class French restaurant in London. One could say that Colin was also getting ready for his day. After swilling his way through two to three bottles of wine, he would trundle down to the pub, a five-minute walk down the road. There, he would while away the afternoon and have a productive networking session with others of like mind before heading back home. He was forty-two and no longer able to work on account of his self-inflicted addiction. Much of this he blamed on his in-laws' cellar full of excellent home-brewed boutique wines. Colin barely ate any more, and his slight frame seemed to wither away by the day. He needed a walking stick to steady himself when outside. The drinking had a sedative effect on him; he was always calm and polite despite the copious amounts of alcohol he consumed. Theresa towered beside him; she was stocky and brusque in manner, always loud and aggressive.

'Thank you, Theresa,' he remarked as he shakily raised the glass to his lips.

She snarled back loudly at him, her comment acrimonious as always. Theresa had not shaken off her strong French accent, nor had she adapted to the circumspect ways of the English. What she had done well was master the use of coarse language. When angry, the most outrageously callous and vulgar words would spew forth from her. Sadly, it was far too often. Today did not differ from any other, but what was about to happen was going to put a distinct edge to the already fractured relationship.

Theresa sighed as she put the phone down. The news of her father's death had finally arrived. She had expected it, yet the element of surprise and shock took hold of her and tears welled up in her eyes. She cried quietly, reminiscing. Colin was in the shower when the phone had rung; he emerged, looking fresh and still in his dressing gown. Theresa had composed herself well enough to convey the news to him without breaking down.

Colin hugged Theresa and offered the customary condolences, then sat down at the dining table and shakily poured himself another glass. The fortification it provided was imperative before he could think or say anything further.

'Perhaps you should get down to the restaurant, quickly, you know, to sort things out for when you're away,' he said. 'I can run down to the travel agents, see if we can fly out this evening…or, or…early tomorrow morning.' The words came out more shakily than the wine he'd poured out.

Theresa's family lived in a small village close to the seaside; it was about a hundred kilometres from Nantes, which was the closest airport, not the most convenient for travel. Her mother had passed away three years ago from cancer, the same illness that had now taken her father. Theresa had three brothers and a sister, all married with children and all anxious about the division of the parental property. This comprised a small dairy/poultry farm and vineyard. There had already been substantial bickering about this, so Theresa knew that this would not be a nice affair. Further, there was considerable animosity shown by her siblings towards her 'good for nothing' English husband. Fortunately, Colin remained too drunk to care about how they felt towards him.

'No, I think I'd better go down to the travel agents myself to make sure there is no mess-up,' said Theresa emphatically. 'I can call Maggie and ask her to be in charge at the restaurant for the next week. I also think it's best that you don't come this time, Colin. There will be a lot that I will need to sort out with my family and you know what a problem they can be!'

'Theresa, I will not let you face this alone. I'm going to be by your side when you need me. Isn't that what marriage is all about?' said Colin, leaning across the table and putting his frail arm around her neck.

In all honesty, Colin could not dream of missing out on a trip to France, not when his thoughts lingered on that cellar full of vin rouge just waiting to be drunk. He remembered full well the number of times Theresa had tried to go on her own, using, as he felt, his failing health as an excuse. Without a doubt, though, he was in terrible shape and could barely walk a hundred yards without having to sit down for a rest. Still, he had always had a persuasive argument and won. And in this instance, the reasons for accompanying her were manifold.

'You make me sick, you bloody fool,' she cried out. 'You bloody English. You are only good at telling people what to do, but you can't do anything about your own life. Look at the mess you are in! You can't even go to work because you can't stop drinking and you want to go to France only because my father's cellar is full and you can drink all you want. Don't think you can fool me,' said Theresa as she succumbed to the fact that she had given in once again.

Strangely, despite the frequency of their many arguments and the ferociousness with which Theresa lashed out at Colin, he, in good English spirit, always managed to stay calm and placid. He was going, after all, so he simply poured himself another drink with a smile on his face.

The trip to France went with the customary harangue between the two. It attracted the attention of all those nearby; some were eager to hear what was being said, while others backed off in case they got caught up in any physical violence. There was the bus journey to the tube station, the tube to Heathrow, the plane trip to Paris, the connecting flight to Nantes, and the last lap of the journey by car with Theresa's brother.

It was only during this last segment that Colin and Theresa finally ceased arguing.

Theresa rather violently pushed Colin into the back seat. 'You can shut up and go to sleep now,' she said as she slammed the door on him and settled herself in the front seat alongside her brother, Jean-Pierre; then, slipping into her native French, they conversed about what had to be done.

Pierre was the youngest in the family, he was Theresa's favourite and she liked his wife Bettina as well; she did not get on too well with the others. They were all there at the house: Marcel, the eldest, and his wife Marie; Louis and Katherine; her younger sister Suzette and spouse Henri; and Bettina, Jean-Pierre's wife. The children, ten in all, were playing in the garden, creating an unbearable commotion for such a solemn occasion. There appeared to be no exercise of parental discipline. Not even the older children were admonished in any way. They shrieked and they cried while the adults engaged in discussions about the funeral, and the contents of the will.

It was almost five in the afternoon. The women busied themselves with laying out a light supper and getting the children off to bed. After that, time was theirs. They ate the meal with relish and Colin, always polite, congratulated the ladies for the fine spread, even though he ate sparsely. His wineglass, however, had seen many refills, and he was deliriously happy with the tipple. Colin was soon nodding off, regardless of the heightening crescendo at the table. There was, as expected, serious discontent about the division of the property. It was only brought to an end by the urgent need to get what sleep was possible before tomorrow's funeral. It was scheduled for two in the afternoon and final preparations such as arranging the flowers in the church, organising the food and wine for the wake, had yet to be done in the morning. With Pierre's assistance, Theresa managed to drag Colin to the bedroom and got him in a reclining position; she would have been equally happy to have left him hanging over the dining room chair for the night. As far as she was concerned, Colin was about as dead as her father. With utmost relief, she slipped into bed and shut her eyes; sleep overcame her almost immediately.

Morning arrived too soon. Theresa showered and rushed to the kitchen, where Bettina was getting breakfast ready. Pierre had already filled the Aga stove with coal and the kitchen was warm and inviting. Between the three of them, they polished off a baguette and half a dozen croissants fresh from the local bakers. Colin and the children were still asleep and left undisturbed, agreed as being in the best interests of all. Theresa wrote a note to Colin stating that they were off to the undertakers. He was to ensure that the children had breakfast, washed, and changed into the clothes laid out for them in the back room. Everyone would be back around eleven, when the neighbours were expected to arrive to pay their last respects.

The remains of Monsieur Pailly lay at the undertakers for his friends and relatives to visit one last time. This was a small village where everyone knew each other and the occasion brought together friend and foe alike. In due time, the cortège moved to the little church on the hill, where a brief service was held before they buried Monsieur Pailly alongside his wife. The crowd meandered slowly back to the house to celebrate his life with food and drink.

Theresa was beginning to feel both the physical and emotional strain of the occasion. The noise, the children and the constant pouring of drinks and serving of food were draining her energy. She was relieved to see that Colin had held up so far and was, in fact, keeping the children under control. Even more so, the children appeared immensely amused by whatever he was saying to them; they were listening intently. All the better for everyone. And at least Colin was keeping himself out of trouble!

With formalities at an end, the family sat down for a bite to eat. They were all exhausted, relieved that all had gone well but very much anxious now about the division and transfer of property. Marcel was the first to speak and, being the eldest, held the view that he had the first choice. His prime antagonist was Louis, who argued that Marcel had shown no interest whatsoever in the farm. Suzette claimed she was in greatest need as her husband was eternally unemployed, and that was how it all started.

Theresa butted in when she could no longer contain herself. She had sacrificed much by going to London to earn better money to support her parents and save the farm. But her words were more to support her brother Jean-Pierre, who had been the farm's prime worker. 'Enough of all this argument,' she said. 'We all know that our parents wanted all of us to have an equal share in this property, but we can't do that unless we sell everything first and then divide up the money. So let's see how many of us want to sell the property. Why don't we have a vote on this? So, who is for selling?'

Silence ensued for the first time, but only for a moment.

There were no takers for selling, but Marcel spoke out. 'Selling is out of the question. Our parents never wanted us to sell this property and we can easily divide the land into equal parts, as I have already showed you many a time. Here is the surveyor's report dividing this land into five allotments. It was of course our parents' wish that I, being the oldest, would inherit the house and carry on the family tradition.'

The sight of the surveyor's report resulted in an instantaneous outburst from everyone. They all knew that the surveyor was a good friend of Marcel. Undoubtedly, the division benefited Marcel. Louis, being a builder, knew full well that future developments proposed for the area would soon devalue the farmland, but not the land on which the house stood. He was not going to stand for Marcel's plan; he made his point clear by bringing his fist down hard on the table. Henri was all for getting quick cash and kept pushing Suzette to demand a sale of the property. Pierre felt more and more helpless and at the mercy of the others. Farming had been his entire life, and without the land and a home for his family, he would be lost.

Everyone voiced their opinions at the same time. The noise in the dining room had reached an unbearable crescendo, broken only when Suzette directed their attention to a so far ignored member of the party.

It was none other than Colin, the always cheerful, always ditsy tipsy Colin, wanting his say in the matter. Once a measure of quiet had been achieved and all eyes focused on him, he embarked on his speech. Colin knew clearly what he wished to say. He also knew that the reception he would get would be undermined by his shaky voice and unstable stance. He stood up, glass in hand, and acknowledged everyone around the table with a nod.

With his other hand resting on Theresa's shoulder for support, he started. 'Let me begin by paying my last respects to Monsieur Pailly, my father-in-law. Yes, Monsieur Pailly was certainly, I would say, the best father-in-law a man could have had. In the beginning, we had our differences of course, none too serious and really no more than the usual cross Channel differences, language and culture mostly. But Monsieur Pailly soon found out that, though I was English, I had a very refined palate for wine, a palate which could discern the most distinguished wine from that which did not quite make the mark. I'm referring here to those "not quite good enough" wines that are easily mistaken to be the best by so many of the finest wine tasters.' (Colin was very prone to bragging about himself.) 'Even in the last years of his illness, he would welcome Theresa and me, always with open arms, by opening not just any old bottle, but the best bottle of wine from his cellar. To me, this was the biggest compliment Monsieur Pailly could ever pay me as an Englishman. Let us now raise our glasses in a toast to Monsieur Pailly.'

Everyone raised their glasses to 'Monsieur Pailly' with little conviction.

Colin raised his hand to indicate that he had not yet finished, then cleared his throat and carried on in a slow and stuttering fashion. 'While I acknowledge that I am an outsider to the family, Monsieur Pailly had a great deal of respect for me, in particular my business acumen. He often sought my advice on many matters, and he took that advice very, very seriously indeed. Yes, I know that most of you are unaware of this, but your father and I were working on plans to develop this property, into a multimillion-euro tourist resort.' Then, looking at Theresa. who was eyeing him dangerously and aggressively as were the others, he carried on, 'Yes, darling, I know I mentioned nothing to you about this, but your father wanted to perfect the plan, which it almost is now, before putting the idea to everyone. With the sad and untimely death of Monsieur Pailly, it is my duty to now unveil to you his plans for all of us, and I will do so in due course. But let me reassure you that this, this is going to be the best thing that could happen to any of us, and before we know it, we're all going to be millionaires,' said Colin with a look of unrestrained pride. 'Yes, that's right, millionaires.'

'Colin, are you being a stupid idiot again?' thundered Theresa. 'How come none of us heard not so much as a whisper of this multimillion-euro plan, and where or what is it, anyway? Now that our father has passed away, can you tell us about this wonderful plan that only you know of? You make me sick, you silly man,' she said and with that, she knocked his arm off her shoulder. 'I knew that bringing you on this journey would only be trouble.'

Colin lost his balance, fumbled and fell over, together with his chair.

'Stay down there and keep your mouth shut, you idiot,' she said, refusing to help him up as he pleaded for a lift with his outstretched arm.

Suzette was distressed and got up to assist him.

Theresa quickly cut that short. 'Don't worry about him, Suzette. It will shut him up for a while. We have enough things to discuss and sort out without Colin trying to be the problem-solver. He can get himself up and have another drink,' said Theresa, placing an almost full bottle of wine on the floor, beside the pitiful frame that now lay moaning and groaning on the floor.

Talk resumed around the table. Colin's groans soon became inaudible as the uproar in the room increased. Marcel's plan quickly lost support. It was not the idea that was the problem, rather the fact that it was Marcel's friend who had drawn up the plan. Suzette and Louis were more in favour of selling the entire property, and so was Theresa, a view which directly opposed that held by Colin. Pierre suggested a subdivision by an unknown third party, and so it went on, and on. It was the chiming of the old grandfather clock that made them realise how much time they had spent trying to reach a simple decision. It was midnight and suddenly, Theresa and everyone else around the table went silent. All eyes focused on the space which had initially been occupied by Colin.

Colin lay motionless on the floor, a tangled mess, with his chair partly on top of him. His body was slightly twisted as he had tried to cling onto the arm of the chair in an attempt to haul himself up.

'Colin, what's the matter with you?' said Theresa with genuine concern as she bent down and shook him on the shoulder; she hoped to goodness that he was in a mere drunken stupor.

His body had lain sprawled on the floor, a limp, lifeless-looking mass for four hours! Fear overwhelmed her and the rest of the family. Had her blow sent Colin to his death? No, that would be impossible. He was simply too full of the grog, just sleeping it off. Still, one could never be sure.

Theresa took his left wrist and tried to feel for a pulse. Her relief was immense as she looked up at all those concerned faces looking down at her. The heartbeat was there, but decidedly weak. His face was ashen and looked deathly.

'He's okay,' she informed them hoarsely. 'Someone, quickly ring for the ambulance. Tell them that he is unconscious and I think he must have lost a lot of blood internally. Look at how grey his face looks! I can't believe that we ignored him for nearly four hours. Yes, for almost four hours he has been lying here unconscious. I'm afraid that the doctors are going to question us about this. What do you think we should tell them when they ask us what happened?' Her voice was hushed.

As matters progressed, it was not just the doctors asking questions, but the police as well.

Colin lay sedate and demure in his hospital bed, secretly enjoying the magnitude of concern from his wife and her family, something he rarely received. He had a fractured tibia, the larger long bone extending from the knee to the ankle, and three broken ribs as a result of the fall. The doctors, nurses and ambulance staff were appalled when the details relating to the accident slowly but surely emerged. Theresa, in particular, and her family were treated with the greatest disdain, and not without good reason, for the internal bleeding could easily have led to Colin's demise. Theresa did her utmost to avoid meeting the doctors when she visited Colin in hospital. They made offensive and snide remarks to her that insinuated ulterior motives on her part.

Colin for once had all the care and attention he could desire. The nurses fussed around him, and he certainly had his eye on one or two. Youthful frolics, jokes and laughter surrounded him. Even Theresa's family had changed their tune towards him; kind words were spoken, and flowers and fruit were brought to him daily. So, although Colin was in pain, he was enjoying the whole charade of everyone being nice to him for a change.

Theresa was overwhelmed by the multitude of problems facing her. There was the real possibility of Colin making a big thing of this and filing a complaint to the police, and then there was the problem of getting back to London with Colin in such a severely disabled state. She had already had several confrontations with the airline, now refusing to take Colin on board, given his current state. They indicated very firmly to Theresa that the liability was far too great. To cap it all, Theresa's firm was not obliging her with any more time off work; and travelling to London by other means was nigh on impossible, considering Colin's condition.

'No, madam, it is quite impossible for us to take Mr Whitehead on board to London this Thursday. The doctor's report states clearly that he is unfit to travel,' stated the airline receptionist calmly for about the fourth time.

'Listen, you,' said Theresa, by now all fired-up and indignant, 'I know what the doctor has said and I am sick of hearing you say it to me again and again. I've already told you more than once that I have to be in London by Friday at the latest. If I don't get there, perhaps I won't have a job any more.'

'Yes, madam, I do understand and please try to understand that I'm not trying to create a problem for you but our policy guidelines clearly state…'

Theresa knew how to be ugly when things did not go her way. 'Mademoiselle, I am aware of your policy guidelines,' interrupted Theresa brusquely, 'but don't you think that there are exceptions you have to deal with at times? That is what service is all about. Now that you are faced with such a problem, perhaps you should be thinking of how to get around this situation, not talking about what your policy says. Let me make this clear to you, if my husband and I don't fly to London this Thursday, I will talk to your most senior manager, and who knows, perhaps after that, you won't be sitting at this desk looking pretty!' said Theresa, almost hoarse with all the shouting.

The travel agent was visibly shaking with fear of Theresa's menacing look and tone of voice. There was always a nasty person to deal with, but this one had really got her near the brink of tears. In a quivering voice, she managed to tell Theresa that she would speak with her boss at once and try to find a positive solution. She would get back to Theresa as soon as her boss returned from her lunch break. Theresa obliged her with a thunderous look and stormed out of the office.

Thursday was about as hectic as the day of the funeral. Property matters remained unsettled as they said goodbyes. Some were tearful and others not. Theresa felt very much for Pierre, Bettina and their three children, and she was anxious about how they would fare over the eventual division. Her own fate had never been of much concern to her. She was content with her lot, even her drunken husband, Colin. It was time for the journey home and, much to Theresa's delight, the airline had gone as far as organising an ambulance with two paramedics to drive her and Colin to the airport. The same service was being made available at the other end. Gratefully, Theresa acknowledged the leniency being shown by the airline and apologised to the young agent for her harsh words. It was difficult for her to accept the fact that her behaviour had been out of line, but that summed up Theresa in a nutshell, always mercurial and temperamental.

As Colin was being carried into the ambulance on a stretcher, Theresa gave him the sternest of looks. 'I don't know why the hell I married you, you bastard,' she said, in an accent which was increasingly becoming more French than English. So harsh was her tone that even the paramedics and family members could not resist raising their eyebrows. 'I did not want you on this journey in the first place, but you got around me with all your stupid talk about being by my side. All you want is your drink and a good time. And what's the point of all the showing off? Trying to make out that you had some secret plan with my father that none of us know about…?'

'Yes, Theresa, I know I got carried away a bit, but you know I meant no harm…'

'No harm indeed. You interfere with the family affairs, making everyone angry, and then end up a bloody mess on the floor…'

Having landed at Heathrow Airport, Theresa was relieved to see the paramedics and ambulance waiting to take them to the hospital.

'Do you realise what a lot of trouble you have caused? I could have made this journey to France and back with only half the arguments I had with my family, not to mention all the problems I had with the airline to get you on this flight. This journey has been nothing but a nightmare for me. My father must be looking at me now and laughing, laughing at the idiot I married. I bet he's had a much better journey going to the other side than we've had, eh? What do you think, you idiot?'

They had arrived at London Hospital; the formalities were soon completed, and they assigned Colin a bed in the men's ward overlooking the busy main road. It was an immense relief to Theresa, who planned on going straight on to work from the hospital.

The bus journey to work took longer than expected due to traffic hold-ups. As Theresa disembarked, her phone rang. It was the matron from Colin's ward. In a curt voice that was laced with annoyance, she told Theresa that when the doctor arrived to inspect Colin, Colin had disappeared from his hospital bed. Quite extraordinary, as he was bedridden. A search had been organised, and the police had been informed. It transpired that Colin had 'borrowed' his neighbour's wheelchair, exited the hospital and, having crossed the extremely busy six-lane road, had made his way to the pub, where he was found finishing a pint of ale. Matron informed Theresa that if such a thing happened again, the hospital would dismiss Colin immediately; beds were in short supply and they could do without the likes of Colin. So the drama had not ended.

It was a subdued yet undeniably happy Theresa who made her way back to the hospital a week later to collect Colin. He was by then well accustomed to moving around with his crutches, and the ward matron was overtly joyous to release her charge on him. Theresa had gone to see Colin midweek and during that visit, he had in a perfectly sober state of mind divulged something astonishing to her. Before Theresa's mother passed away, both parents had discussed and written a new will, with Colin having the power of attorney. While the family had always subscribed to a frugal lifestyle, the Paillys had over time acquired substantial property holdings that none of the children were aware of. They eventually sold this package of property off at a premium price of five million euro, which now sat in a Swiss bank account in Theresa's name. The parents had always recognised Theresa as the person who had made their initial investments possible. They had no wish to deal with the confrontation that this bequest would initiate from the rest of the family and thus had preferred it to remain silent until both had passed away. Now that the parents were gone, Theresa would have access to the Swiss bank account and the parental home and the small block of land on which it stood. The farm, vineyard and several other properties the Paillys owned in the nearby locale were to be divided equally among the rest of the children. There were two copies of the new will, one at the Swiss Bank and another at Barclays Bank in London; it ensured complete secrecy until the very end.

Colin had not had the time to access the will from Barclays Bank before they left for France but now, he was able to leave all of that to Theresa, who had confirmed its existence; another tall tale from Colin was the last thing she needed. There would be no ifs or buts now; everything was clearly laid out.

Theresa could hardly believe that Colin had kept all of this under wraps for almost four years; he didn't seem as worthless to her now. They could both look forward to a fresh start. And what of the haggling brothers and sister? Hopefully, la Manche would prove itself a sufficient physical barrier to keep them apart.

Pie in the Sky

It had been a mammoth move from London for Peter and me, with two young children aged two and four in tow. This was 1988, and Brisbane was still a place unknown to many from the western hemisphere. That arrival came with several surprises. The intensity of the Queensland sun as we disembarked from the carrier felt ferocious. I looked in all directions; not a single cloud blotted the brilliant blue of that sky; it stretched endlessly in every direction. The land seemed to stretch out to the horizon. Little stood in its way apart from the patches of green interspersed by patches of brown; so few buildings, not what I expected of a city. And then there was the airport itself, a multi-purpose hangar that accommodated arrivals, departures, customs and immigration, baggage and quarantine, plus everything else in the one small space. It was unsettling to see no other plane on that rough dirt track which was the runway. What a far cry this was from what we had left behind for good.

The shock was short-lived; our moods lifted up as the taxi drove us past Brisbane River, along Breakfast Creek. The water was a dazzling blue, and the sun beating down on it made it glisten like a burst of stars floating over its surface. This was indeed a feast for the eyes. It's a vision that I always look forward to seeing, each time I return to Brisbane from a trip.

I first met Joanne on our second day in Brisbane as newly arrived immigrants. We needed a place to stay, and I had a list of real estate agents to visit. I had no choice but to take the children along with me. It was winter, yet the sun was unbearably scorching and our pallid skins were already tanning. The children wearied quickly from the heat so we decided on ice cream to cool ourselves down; then, very arduously, I resumed what appeared to be a fruitless search. Directions led me to an agency off the beaten track; in fact, I would never have found it had instructions not been provided.

The building was large and expansive and on the main road; finding the way in was not that straightforward. The stairway was tucked far inside a dingy-looking arcade. It was the sort of arcade where one would not expect to find anything remotely pleasant. I hesitated to venture forth and entered only because there was nothing else on my list, and finding a roof over our heads was imperative. We were exhausted and dragged ourselves up the stairs. I had to carry my younger child, who at this stage adamantly refused to walk. I could see that this had once been a grand building; the signs of decay and damp were now clearly visible. Patches of grey mould adorned the walls.

Joanne greeted me at the entrance. She was the face of the business, sitting close to the door; she was middle-aged and plump, with lots of poorly applied make-up. It did not enhance her appearance. There was a smell of perfume, rather like jasmine, but mixed with the smell of the blistered plaster peeling off the walls, its utility was lost. My eyes were drawn to the chunky beads adorning Joanne's neck; they unduly emphasised her large, heaving bosom. Joanne's face resembled that of a moon in its roundness and she had done her dark brown hair up in a bun; it was held together by a large, bejewelled clasp. She wore a long-sleeved floral shirt and several rings on both hands, all in the same style as her necklace. I found her manner of speech rather loud and abrupt before discovering later that this was 'the real Aussie' way with words. Then, I saw the compassion on her face; she kept moving her gaze from me to the children and back; I could see that her mind was working nineteen to the dozen. Joanne was infinitely generous, and Joanne was determined that, come hell or high water, she was going to find us a place to rent. Officially, she had nothing in the books to offer me, but she said she had some contacts and was soon busy on the phone. She found a place for us, and thereupon began an enduring friendship.

A few years down the track, our financial situation had improved. We talked about moving to a larger house, possibly buying in a nicer suburb.

I called Joanne to discuss what was available; she was more than overjoyed about showing me a few properties that fitted our requirements. We made the arrangement for Wednesday and I met her around mid-morning at her office. Our tour of properties was going to take us past a particular pie shop where Joanne intended to buy her supper for that evening.

She swooned over the quality of the pies at this outlet, swearing them to be the best in Brisbane. 'Caroline, I swear to God, the pies in this shop are absolutely out of this world. You'll find nothing better in all of Queensland. They are just divine. God, my mouth is already watering just thinking about them. You really must try one. If you don't, you won't know what you're missing.'

'Hm…the kids love the meat pies that I make myself, but I might well be tempted to buy one for a change.' But then pies were not my interest on this trip. I simply looked forward to see a few pleasant houses that would be within our budget.

I followed Joanne to the car park which was on the roof of the building. We clattered up a flight of stairs and made a brief stop to chat to the manageress of the op-shop on the floor above.

Once outside the shop, Joanne was quick off the mark to rave about the merchandise in the store by way of recommendation to me. 'This is where I shop so that I can stay upmarket and well dressed for my job. You know, it's very important to look good when your job involves meeting so many members of the public.'

'Yes, they certainly have some nice things for sale,' I said, looking around and trying to find something I could comment on positively. 'I do like this jewellery, very nice indeed.'

My opinion on Joanne's op-shop attire rated it as rather out of date and decidedly dowdy, and I couldn't help noticing the smudge of lipstick on her upper lip. Our opinions about appearance differed considerably. I wondered how I would feel about the pie. I hoped her rating of food would be different. We left the shop.

We walked through a short passage and then up some rather steep steps to the rooftop. The stairs were narrow, and Joanne manoeuvred them sideways. She was puffing and heaving, taking each step slowly and carefully, finally giving a long-awaited sigh of relief as she reached the end of the climb. She stopped for a few deep breaths. The redness of her cheeks slowly eased, and she stopped panting. The telltale sign was easy to spot. She was a heavy drinker. The rooftop landing had space for only nine or ten cars.

'This climb's a bit of a shocker. Pity there's no lift to get us up here,' said Joanne once she had recovered and was breathing normally.

'Hm, it is rather steep. Is this the only car parking that you can use? Might be easier to park somewhere else, perhaps…?' I remarked, noticing the strain that it had been for Joanne.

'No, this is it. I'm not going to pay when I have free parking here.'

I noticed that her walking pace had slowed considerably. She headed towards the far corner and I kept alongside.

'Here's my beauty,' she remarked as she walked towards the driver's side of the tiniest little Suzuki that I had ever set eyes upon. It was beaten-up, scratched and rusty; what one would call an old bomb.

Joanne was quick to sense my shock. 'Well… it's not the nicest-looking car, but it does get me around, which is what's important. Besides, I've had no one complain about it. I take people around and get them back safely, and I really couldn't afford a new car even if I wanted to get one… So this little baby still serves the purpose. So let's get ourselves organised then.'

I was still dazed at the thought that she carried clients around in this old banger. I opened the passenger door, and my jaw dropped. There was not a chance of finding any sitting space in either front or back seats. And the odour that hit my nostrils was an absolute turn-off; it was a mix of rust, dust, mould, sweat and all things unpleasant. No wonder Joanne talked about 'getting organised'. The car was packed to the brim. There was a vacuum cleaner in the back and no end of other clutter which ranged from saucepans to buckets, piles of newspapers and magazines, and dustbin bags of old clothes, all of which had to be moved and shoved around, so that I could have a parasite-laden front seat to sit upon. There was little that could be done about the unpleasant pong apart from hoping that it would blow away. I sank most uncomfortably into the well-used seat and attempted to do up the seatbelt; it was so mangled that it really served no purpose.

Seeing me settled, Joanne hopped across to the driver's side, buckled herself and turned the ignition. She heaved a very audible sigh of relief when the engine spluttered and started. And then we were on our way. I sincerely hoped that this was not the sort of vehicle that other real estate agents in Brisbane used for their clients. It wasn't, as I later found out; Joanne was simply one of those 'one in a million' eccentrics.

The plan was that we would first view the properties that were closest to the city, and then radiate to the outer suburbs. It was a frustrating journey, seeing houses in such disrepair, ill-kept and so high-priced. I was not new to buying real estate, but regardless, despondency crept in. There were better bargains to be had farther outside the city bounds, and there were a couple that deserved a second look. I made note of them. Peter and I could view them on another day.

We were tottering along towards the southern suburbs of Brisbane and as we turned into Cavendish Road, Joanne could no longer contain her excitement.

'It's a few blocks down,' she said rather excitedly to me, her forlorn passenger. 'I'll show you in a minute.'

'What?' I remarked, slightly confused. My mind was on the unsightly houses I had just viewed.

'The pie shop, Caroline, the pie shop!' said Joanne, unable to comprehend how I had so soon forgotten about it.

'Of course, I'm looking forward to seeing the place. It's always good to know where to find good stuff,' I said.

'But first, there's a house I want to show you a little farther down, and on our return, we'll stop over here. I haven't had one of these for ages, and John will be over the moon. And the best thing about this is that I don't have to do any cooking tonight, ha-ha, ha-ha,' said Joanne, tickled by the whole scenario.

I had the secret feeling that Joanne did little cooking on the whole and lots of drinking, red wine in particular, for which she appeared to have a penchant.

We had a look at two houses in fact, before making our way back to the pie shop on Cavendish Road. This was a large and busy street that distilled much of the traffic going south from the city. It appeared to be a road favoured by large trucks, as the traffic moved fairly fast on the wider than average lanes. We had to park on the northbound side and then cross over to the other side.

Once inside the pie shop, Joanne could not stop talking about which pie she was going to have for tea that evening. She was effusive, almost dribbling, and eventually, the choice was made. I abstained, as I thought the pies were rather expensive and I was not a pie fanatic in any case. They smelled very good, though, regardless of the fumes from the trucks outside.

We headed back to the car for our return homewards, mission accomplished for both of us. I had seen quite a few houses, albeit only one or two of them deserved further investigation. And Joanne held her prized possession close to her breast, crooning over it as though it were a newborn babe. She placed the pie very carefully, almost tenderly, on the roof of the car while she went through the ritual of letting me into the passenger seat; we buckled up, ready to go.

I despaired when she turned the key, and the car refused to start. We looked at each other; I could see that this was no surprise to her.

'I wonder if I've got enough gas?' she said. 'It's hard to say. My petrol meter doesn't work and I can't remember when I last got any.' She reached across and opened the glove compartment; it barely needed a tap to spurt out a volume of chewing gum, brochures and bills, among other bits and bobs. She grabbed the bills and started looking through them. 'No, that's not it, that's not it... No, these are too old. I'm sure I got some gas earlier this week...or was it the end of last week? Hmm...' She stuffed everything back in the glove compartment, which now refused to shut at all.

I was dog-tired and wanted to get back home in time to collect the children from school; I found all the delays particularly annoying. I believe Joanne sensed this, as I had gone silent, making only the most mundane of comments.

And then Joanne did the most extraordinary thing. 'Well, it's time for the big bang,' she said. She got out of the car, cranked the bonnet up, came around and opened the passenger door. 'Stay where you are,' she said, as I started to unbuckle my seat belt.

She reached under my seat and pulled out a huge hammer; the head of the hammer had a diameter of about an inch and a half. I certainly would have had an issue lifting such a weight, but for Joanne, who was built like a dwarf Amazonian, it appeared no heavier than a feather.

'Cover your ears,' she cried as she carried it to the front of the car, lifted it high, and then, with all her might, she came down on the engine with it. Bang! The noise reverberated in my ears and the tiny Suzuki swayed from side to side.

'That should do it,' she said.

The hammer went back where it came from. Joanne was in the car again and buckled up. She turned on the ignition. The magic had worked and the little car was purring, and ready to go.

'It always works,' said Joanne, delighted with her trick.

The car eased off into the street and was soon speeding along, keeping pace with the fast-moving traffic.

We would easily have done a kilometre when Joanne, to my utter confusion, threw an absolute panic.

'My pie, my pie, oh no! my meat pie! It's just flown off the roof, Caroline. I forgot my meat pie.'

I looked over my shoulder. But by then it was just a blob of a flying saucer landing on the tarmac in the distance. Brakes were applied instantly, and we came to a screeching halt. I'm quite certain that Joanne paid no attention to the traffic conditions when she did this, so we were indeed lucky to be in one piece. Then, to my amazement and despite the heavy traffic, she started weaving her way back in reverse gear to retrieve her meat pie.

'Joanne, you don't think you'd be able to eat the pie, do you? Look at all the trucks – they're bound to have run over it by now and if not, it's going to be in a million pieces anyway.'

Joanne's face was set firm. 'I'm not going home without my meat pie! I've paid for it and I'm going to eat it one way or the other.'

It was an adamant, almost childlike statement of utter determination; it took me by surprise.

By this time, we had reached the approximate vicinity of the pie which, after its unexpected flight, lay in the middle lane with packaging slightly unravelled; it was difficult to say from where we were whether a passing vehicle had run it over or not.

I had not the slightest idea whether Joanne's rust bucket on four wheels had anything called emergency lights, but we were now parked on the edge of the left lane of a bustling three-lane highway. Joanne was out of the car in a flash. Her eyes darted this way and that. Through the window she showed me her tightly crossed fingers. As soon as there was a pause in the traffic, she rushed to the middle lane, scooped up what was left of her pie, and zigzagged her way back into the car, clinging tightly to her precious cargo. This was strenuous exercise for her and her podgy red face looked ready to burst. She was gasping, and I could hear her heartbeat. Her hands were shaking as she handed the rescued package to me in slow motion. I felt panicky and speechless. I waited tensely, expecting her to collapse with exhaustion. A heart attack, perhaps. Then, very slowly, she looked me straight in the eye and her face broke into a beaming smile. I felt a moment of ecstatic relief.

'Look.' she said. 'My pie! It's fine! John and I are going to feast on this tonight.' All had ended well for Joanne as far as her meat pie was concerned.

I looked at the crumpled heap on my lap and tried as best as I could to break the news gently to her. 'Joanne, I think your pie has been run over. Look at the state it's in, and you can see tyre marks over here.' I pointed them out to her. 'Perhaps you'll have to throw this away after all.'

'Nonsense! It may be in a mess but it's still going to taste good.'

I decided it was best to say no more about the pie and focused on small talk until we were back in the city.

Other things made me temporarily forget the day's events. Come dinner time. though, there was much talk and laughter about the eccentric Aussie by the name of Joanne. The bounds of professionalism may not have been Joanne's strong point, although, without doubt, endless fun and entertainment awaited those not confined by time and straitjacketed by how things ought to be done. Speaking for myself, she had turned the odious task of house hunting into a day of fun and frolic; a day of adventure with a person who will never be forgotten.

An Oyster Hunt Gone Awry

'*Bonjour*, my friend… How are you, my dear Sophie? I told you I would visit you someday so here I am, even though I can't believe I have made it. At long last anyway…he, he, he.' Yvette's Frenchness reverberated through her accent.

My friend of many decades was at long last fulfilling her dream of visiting me in my new home Down Under. The passing of time had not changed her one iota; she waved frantically and shouted out loud as I pulled up at the airport terminal.

It was a glorious day in Brisbane, marred only by my concerns; would I, or for that matter my family, cope with three weeks of Yvette? Having known her for many years in London, I knew that this was going to be a visit that I would not forget.

True enough, Yvette lived up to her usual form.

Yvette still emphasised the wrong part of words and sentences and, as always, kept on talking without the need for a breather. She was a widow and enjoyed being single once again. Her short-lived relationship with an English husband had been one long cat and dog fight. She enjoyed her freedom and doing exactly what she wanted. Yvette looked very much the tomboy. Her dark hair was cropped short as usual and her pallid white skin contrasted with my tan. She was much taller than me and had put on some weight since I last saw her.

We got home, and I walked Yvette through the front door. Unsurprisingly, she tripped over the doormat and fell flat on her face. Ten minutes later, the wine glass she had in hand adorned my carpet with a rosy pink pattern. Yes, it was the same Yvette, but what I found most difficult to cope with was her loud and incessant talking; it provided no respite for retort or response.

'So, Yvette, have you thought of what you'd like to do during this visit?'

'Ah, yes, I read something about…is it the Coast of Gold? They say it is exquisite, and you know how I like the seaside, so I would like to go there if I can. Maybe we can even catch some fish, eh? He, he, he.'

'I think you mean the Gold Coast. Yes, it's fabulous and about an hour south of us. We could drive there one day.'

Although I am no fan of that part of the state, Yvette wished to see the Gold Coast; I felt obliged to take her there.

We set off one morning around nine. Yvette talked nineteen to the dozen while I drove southbound on the freeway with my ears closed; I had to maintain my sanity. In many ways, Yvette and I had little in common, making it a rather difficult relationship. We had been work colleagues, visited each other occasionally, and moved on; except Yvette was still hanging on to me. She, as always, did the talking and I did the listening, although mostly, only just.

I turned left off the coastal road and then left again into a broad drive alongside a row of large, ostentatious houses. I made it a point to stop at a beach well short of Surfer's Paradise. A beach that was quiet and serene, devoid of tourists and magnificently beautiful; this small suburb was called Runaway Bay. It was the haven of the rich, the nearby yacht club a sure indicator of the wealth.

Across a short stretch of green lay the most stupendous sight. The sea was as blue as the cloudless sky above. A small promontory protected the bay from the fury of the Pacific Ocean. The vividness and depth of colour were breathtaking. The picture-postcard scenario truly took Yvette aback

'Oh, my God! It's beautiful. Hurry up, Sophie, let's get down to the beach. That water looks so inviting. The fish are waiting for us, he, he, he.'

We gathered our towels and hurried across the sand-drenched grass. The wind blew hard on our faces, taking my hair in all directions. It was no bother for Yvette. Her hair was cropped to her scalp. We settled down by the rocky edge that marked the end of the bay before going into the water. Yvette was still talking non-stop as we spread our towels and sat down to take in the view and the fresh air. I simply wished hard that she would stop her noisy blabber. To obliterate it, I closed my eyes to enjoy the sun and breeze.

And then, as if in answer to my silent prayer, Yvette suddenly did go quiet. It was a moment so bizarre that I opened my eyes seeking clarification.

When she began speaking, it was in tones of hushed excitement. 'Sophie! I can't believe it. Can you see those oysters…there, on the rocks? I have to get them,' she said.

My eyes looked hard in the direction she pointed at and saw nothing. But she was desperate for them. The yearning was in her eyes, and with a starved and hungry look on her face, she jumped up and set off on her sacred mission to harvest those oysters.

By the time I got to the edge of the rocks, she was almost halfway down the cliff edge. While not a particularly hard descent, we were both near sixty and had back and knee problems. I was certainly not going to risk my back for anything.

'Be careful, Yvette,' I cried out, just as she slipped down the rocky embankment before falling into the water.

She hoisted herself up with a small rock in hand. Aiming it at the oysters, she lunged towards the rock face. 'Oh shit, I didn't get it.' Time for another try.

I fretted as I saw Yvette lose her balance. She twisted her body to regain it, but in doing so her foot slipped and she went face down into the water.

'Yvette, please be careful…, I don't think those oysters are worth it,' I implored as I bit my lip in concern for her safety.

Yvette had always been a clumsy person and to my horror, just as I thought she was getting herself together, she lost her balance once again and went crashing into the water face down for the second time. The water was shallow but deep enough to cover her completely; what concerned me were the rocks below. There she was flapping her arms around, much like a fish out of water; it felt like an eternity. Eventually, she hoisted herself up, clothes all dripping and clinging to her body. There were cuts on her arms, her face and her legs, and within minutes the blood started to drip profusely.

Undeterred, she turned round and made her way to the rock face yet again. Picking up another stone, she tried once more to unhinge the oysters. All the while I was pleading for her to forget the oysters and come back up, but she had no ears for me. Her face was set with determination.

'I can't get these bloody oysters to come off. Have you got a knife or something sharp, Sophie?'

'No, I don't… the only thing I have is a teensy-weensy knife in my Swiss card, but it's in the car.'

'Can you get it for me? I'm not going away, you know, until I have the oysters,' said Yvette defiantly.

Knowing there was no way to lure Yvette out of the water, I made my way back to the car in haste. The knife was deplorably small, very much a worthless tool for this occasion.

'I don't think you can do much with this,' I said as I stepped onto a firm rock below and stretched out to pass the knife to Yvette, who had climbed up halfway.

She was ecstatic and, in her haste, and for the third time, she ended up face down in the water. I panicked, thinking she might stab herself with the little knife, thoughts that would never bother Yvette in a million years. She rose out of the water and took her frustration out on the oysters, digging and hacking at them for all she was worth. Sadly, it was all in vain; the oysters turned out to be dead, mere dried-out shells. It was a beaten and forlorn Yvette who climbed back up to lick her wounds. Drenched to the skin and cold, blood dripping down her arms and face and with a badly lacerated knee, things did not look good. I had to focus on how to stop her knee bleeding. It had a deep cut and the entire leg was swelling by the minute.

Yvette stripped down to her bra, and we used her blouse to bandage her knee. I ran back to the car and fetched what first aid I had in the glove compartment; it was pretty useless for a situation such as this. The band-aids were useful for the small abrasions, but it was the knee that was a major concern.

The wind had picked up, and Yvette was shivering in her wet clothing. I decided it best that we get back to the car, where there were dry towels at least, although there was nothing for Yvette to change into, apart from her unused swimwear.

Forlorn with the morning's activity, we gathered our belongings and hobbled back to the car. I opened the rear door nearest the pavement to act as a screen, behind which Yvette could change. As we were near the dead end of the drive, I calculated this to be adequate protection from being seen by vehicles coming towards us. That was a misjudgement. A car came towards us, and no, it did not park. As it swung round the end of the road, the occupants had a full uncensored rear view of Yvette, in the nude.

'Get in the car, Yvette, there's a car behind you,' I cried out to a totally unconcerned Yvette.

The two young men sitting in the car seemed delighted with the spectacle. I could see the looks of glee on their faces and tried to shield Yvette as much as I could with my body. The car made its way to the top of the drive, turned round and came back towards us for a second viewing. Could I blame them?

Yvette changed into her bikini, the only dry clothes she had, and then wrapped a towel around her waist. The challenge had taken a toll on her exuberance.

'Is there a shop nearby?' she enquired. 'I think I'll have to buy some clothes before we go anywhere.'

There was a small shopping mall nearby with a cheap clothing outlet called Best & Less. It was about a five-minute drive away and once inside the shop, I guided Yvette towards the women's clothing section. I left her to her own devices while I had a quick browse myself. It came as no surprise to me to find her towel lying on the floor. But where was Yvette? Yvette was busy trying on clothes and happily strutting around the store in her bikini. I could only sigh. She was French, after all!

She decided on a T-shirt and pair of shorts, which she kept on as we walked towards the counter to pay. It amazed me that Yvette remained so upbeat. Her natter and raucous laughter rang loud and clear; it made us the centre of attraction in the store. All and sundry made their way towards us, curious about the commotion. And there was more embarrassment in store for me.

'How are they going to scan my clothes? I'd better make this easy for them, he, he, he,' she remarked, and with that statement, she hoisted her lumbering self onto the conveyer belt and sailed on to the cashier, laughing herself silly all the way.

People in the queue looked on astonished; I kept my head down sheepishly.

'Hey, I thought I would make this easy for you,' she said to the cashier, who was completely taken aback. In silence, she hastily completed the transaction.

I escorted Yvette out of the shop in a furious rage, feeling comfortable only once we were well away from the shop. We sat down to have some cheesecake and coffee. Yvette could not stop lamenting about the oysters. The sight of them had whetted her appetite; she could talk of nothing else. Her leg was looking terrible, but she showed no concern about it.

'I don't want to worry about my leg…I came here to have a good time. It will get better… Why do you look so worried, Sophie?' she remarked.

Oysters were what mattered. It was very characteristic of Yvette to be fixated on something for inordinately long periods of time. I knew I would have to do something about the situation. It was the best reason I could find to suggest a trip to Sydney, for the prime purpose of visiting the fish market.

We flew in one morning, booked into our hotel, and then took the light rail, alighting near the market. It was immensely crowded as usual. We walked around to have a look before settling down to a late lunch. The barramundi was always my choice. Yvette was nearly choking at the sight of the oysters; she had a massive plateful. This was true fulfilment for her and, I believe, the highlight of her trip to Australia. It was the first time she had ceased to prattle on about every inconsequential thing that entered her mind. For me, this was perhaps the most arduous meal I'd ever sat through. There was Yvette slurping and sucking oysters with both hands at work, and creating an ugly mess all around her plate. It was just like watching a two-year-old eat. She had an enormous appetite and as she was enjoying the meal so much, I bought her another plate. Her face lit up like the sun.

'Yvette, you take your time and enjoy it. I'll just have a look at the delicatessen,' I said as I walked away from the disaster zone and my dear friend Yvette, who was as happy as a pig wallowing in poo.

Two more weeks of this! *Merde!*

'Why, then the world's mine oyster, Which I with sword will open' – William Shakespeare, *The Merry Wives of Windsor*

A Pacific Affair

The rains were ebbing, and the villagers were emerging out of their mud hut dwellings to assess and repair the damage that the monsoon had brought; it was the same each year. The women had gathered at the Red Cross office to collect their rations of provisions, food and medicines to fight minor ailments such as fevers and diarrhoea, so common to this tropical region of Fiji. Yet there was more than the usual flutter of excitement at the centre; there was talk that two young women from Australia were soon to arrive at their village, and what was even more exciting was that they were going to spend three months teaching at the local school. The news spread quickly through the small community and caused so much curiosity that the Red Cross agent had to convene a village meeting to inform and educate the people about this unusual visit. Foremost on the agenda was what this visit would entail in terms of engaging with these two young individuals from a vastly different and affluent nation.

Peter, as Banda was then called since he had been baptised as a Christian, was right amid this at the age of eighteen. His mother was the head of the local school, which boasted an assistant teacher and a classroom that accommodated twenty children. The Red Cross had taken responsibility for the safety of the two visitors and had negotiated with the two teachers to accommodate the girls, one in each house. That evening, Peter's mother addressed her family, who had gathered around her. The major concern was space, where was this young, seventeen-year-old woman going to sleep in their tiny home; they had just two small rooms, which provided sleeping accommodation for the entire family. Peter slept on the floor of his parents' bedroom. His three younger sisters slept in the next room on one large bed and it was there that they decided the visitor would sleep.

When Amelia and Jennifer arrived, the entire village turned up, all in their finery, to welcome their visitors. The children waved little hand-made flags, many running up to the two girls with offerings of flowers. Peter remembered that day as though it were just yesterday. He remembered the bright green frock that Amelia wore, and how it contrasted with the pink shirt and white trousers worn by Jennifer. But most of all he remembered Amelia smiling; it was almost as though she had singled him out of the crowd and was smiling at him alone. The girls were tired after the long trek and they waved furiously at the crowd, before disappearing into the Red Cross Centre where Peter's mother and the assistant teacher were waiting to take over their charges. The excitement decreased, and Peter had work to do with his father. Together, they went into the forest to fell the trees that they would sell at the market the following day.

The evening was full of intense concern about being on best behaviour. Peter's mother and three sisters were in their Sunday best and seated around the small dining table when Peter and his father arrived. The two men washed and changed before joining the rest of the family for the last meal of the day. What began as a formal event soon turned into one full of laughter as the family tried to teach Amelia to eat rice with her fingers, and explain to her that it was common to eat bananas cooked. Peter's family was beginning to feel more comfortable about Amelia fitting into their simple lifestyle, but there was much more that Amelia had to get accustomed to.

The family was quick to notice the look of concern on Amelia's face when she realised she had to share a bed with the three girls. But before long she was in bed, surrounded by Peter's three inquisitive sisters, giggling and laughing with them like their big sister. Peter could remember peeping round the dividing curtain to see the faces of four happy girls playing silly bedtime games. It was a sight that he would not forget in a million years.

The first couple of weeks were challenging for Peter's family, especially his mother, under whose authority Amelia had to undertake her teaching duties. Amelia was amazed at how well the little children spoke English, far better than the adults. They had, through good fortune, been taught by the many missionaries who had visited the village for varying lengths of time.

School began at eight in the morning and concluded at one in the afternoon; They gave the children a meal of rice and vegetables before they returned home. Each morning commenced with a light snack and a glass of milk, and a similar snack was provided at mid-morning. The teachers did not leave the school until around three in the afternoon. They spent the time marking and planning the activities for the next day. Peter's mother and her assistant were glad to have Amelia and Jennifer there; they could take over all the English language classes and organise other craft activities for the children as well. They were also eager to improve their own English by sitting in on Amelia's and Jennifer's classes, and before long everyone had settled into a comfortable routine.

After school, the local families often invited the two girls to taste various delicacies cooked specially for them. Sometimes they would take them to the next village and show them around. Many of the families produced handicrafts such as woven baskets, rugs, mats, hammocks and hats. Fish and game were plentiful. The market was not just a place for trading but also a meeting point for both business and social activities. At the weekend, Amelia and Jennifer would often be found at the market, surrounded by a group of people curious to know about their way of life or eager to practise their English.

Amelia found them to be an inquisitive lot, sometimes asking questions that were extremely personal and invasive but she realised she had to learn to live with it; this was a different culture, and it was her obligation to adapt to her new surroundings. Both girls found the interest that people had in their hair rather flattering and peculiar. Only very few had seen hair that was other than black in colour; although missionaries had come through, few had made their hair visible. So the two girls would sit on the grass giggling and laughing while the young village girls played and braided their hair, intertwining it with flowers and wreaths. Of course, Peter's sisters had first pickings on this highly competitive activity.

It was at the marketplace that Peter approached Amelia and Jennifer, carrying two drinks for the girls. The outer cover of the fruit was orange in colour, and it looked very much like a coconut with the husk on. The top of the husk was cut off to enable the sweet nectar to be drunk; it was this natural sweetness that made it the king of the coconut family. It was on this occasion that Peter invited the two girls to go fishing in the river. Jennifer was quick to notice that Peter could not take his eyes off Amelia, and while he tried to act nonchalant, he took advantage of every occasion to be as near to Amelia and touch her as often as he could.

Banda remembered the private conversation he had had with Amelia that day.

'Would you like to go fishing again tomorrow, Amelia? Just the two of us after school is over? I would like to show you the waterfall further down and we can go for a swim as well.'

'That would be just perfect, Peter. I would love to. I'm glad I brought my swimmers with me,' remarked Amelia.

'Swimmers? I don't think I understand this word. What does it mean?' questioned Peter.

'Oh, I'm sorry, Peter, it means swimsuit. We Aussies like to abbreviate everything, so you're going to hear a lot of strange words from me. But please ask if you don't understand something,' said Amelia reassuringly. 'I think I explained to you what "Down Under" means.'

'Yes, it means Australia.'

'Well, if I say, let's have a barbie, it means let's have a barbecue. And sunglasses are called sunnies and sandwiches are called sandies and it goes on and on,' explained Amelia with a laugh.

'It sounds as if it's not English in some ways,' remarked Peter.

'You're right there. It's only slang. We don't use such words if we're writing something formal.'

The trip to the waterfall was, in every sense, romantic. The water gushed in torrents from what seemed like a grotto of foliage in splendid bloom. It thundered down fearlessly, yet only five hundred metres away it flowed in gentle ripples, clear enough to see the fish and the pebbles at the bottom. Amelia was keenly aware of having roused Peter's feelings. She found him equally exciting, manly for his eighteen years, and handsome. Their eyes met as he gently took her hand and led her into the crystal-clear water. And before they knew what was happening, they were entwined in a deep and lingering kiss. Peter felt that he was in the world of the gods. He had his goddess Amelia in his arms; there was nothing more that he could wish for. No words were needed for him to express his feelings to Amelia, and her response was clear.

They lingered in each other's arms until dusk; Peter played with her long hair, weaving flowers into it. Then he made a wreath of sweet-smelling jasmine flowers, which he placed on her head like a crown. He had called her his princess, and she had thrilled to everything that he had said. Only dusk intervened and made them go home that evening. Peter was not shy to show his feelings towards Amelia in front of his family; they were all excited for them, most of all his three sisters, who kept insisting on asking how it had all happened, and so quickly too.

In truth, Amelia felt rather coy about the openness that seemed expected of her. Once her adopted siblings had fallen asleep, Amelia tip-toed to a corner of the room to call her parents on her mobile. After a few minutes of thought, she decided to leave it till the morning; there was far too much to say and she might well wake up the sleeping family.

Peter's love for Amelia became common knowledge within the community at lightning speed. In many ways, it made things easier for both of them. There was no need for secrecy and meeting after dark. They would spend all their free time in the afternoons walking through the forest, swimming in the river, and doing things that Amelia would normally not have done. Peter knew that Amelia was his one true love, but he feared the future. He knew that the cultural rift would be a problem.

They lived in different countries and then there was Amelia's family. Would they so much as accept him? Could he dare to think of a permanent relationship? He avoided answering that question and decided to leave it in the hands of the gods.

He knew that Amelia was worried too, but she seemed far more at ease, always assuring him that her family was very broad-minded and open to discussion. Amelia spoke a lot about her family. Her parents were both psychologists, and they both worked in family counselling. She also had a sister and brother, both older and studying at university. Although she spoke lovingly of her family accepting their relationship, Peter felt unsure. He wondered how he would get on with Amelia's siblings. The concept of university education was alien to Peter; no one in his village had ever been to university. What would he say to them? Would they scorn him for his lowly status? No end of questions popped up in Peter's mind, and he became restless and moody unless he was in Amelia's reassuring company. But ultimately, he felt it best to leave things to fate.

And the gods did intervene. Amelia's time to head for home was drawing near, and Peter's spirits were at their lowest. He was seated under the mango tree near the school, waiting for Amelia. He saw so much joy on her face as she rushed out of the schoolhouse and ran into his open arms.

'Peter, you aren't going to believe this,' she said.

Peter had just held her close; he could no longer hide his sadness.

'Have a guess,' she said. 'I'll give you three,' she said, with her face beaming.

'Are you going to stay longer in my country?' he questioned.

'No, try again.'

'Are you going to Europe on holiday?' he questioned again.

'No. One more try.'

'I can't,' said Peter.

'All right, I'll tell you,' said Amelia, still looking ecstatic. 'You know I'm leaving next month and neither of us wants to talk about it. Well,

I think we're both going to talk about it a lot because my parents want you to come over and visit Australia.'

'Amelia, you know I don't have money to travel,' said Peter wistfully.

'But you don't have to worry about it. My parents are going to pay for your airfare and everything else. Don't you think it's wonderful?'

Peter was too shocked for words, happy but not knowing how to react to such generosity.

They had walked down to the river with Amelia talking nineteen to the dozen about all the things they were going to do together in Australia. Peter sat listening, asking the occasional question, but needing the time to think things over. The situation overwhelmed him. He would need his parents' permission. Who would help his father if he went? Yet he desired to go. Amelia was good at slowly dispelling his fears. His family, concerned though they were, agreed that he would never have such an opportunity again. So eventually, when Amelia boarded that plane with Jennifer, Peter accompanied them.

*

Meeting Amelia's parents and family was no simple task. Peter felt shy and reserved, concerned about his English and his attire, which was not quite right but that was the easiest of things to fix. It was meeting the family members and friends that created the most stress. They were overly friendly, he felt, trying hard to make him feel at ease; deep inside, he felt that they were putting him on a pedestal so that they could look at him from different angles, critique him, and pass judgement on him. Was he, or was he not, the right partner for Amelia? It was a question that haunted him as well. Somehow, Amelia showed no sign of concern. Neither did her parents.

Curious, thought Peter, putting it down to cultural differences. Amelia had settled into his very humble household so easily, and yet here he was feeling out of place in her home. Her home was a mansion in comparison. He was eternally losing his way around. It had cost Amelia's parents a fair amount of money for his flight and stay. Why had they gone to this trouble over him? Were they sincere, stupid or thoughtless? He voted for the latter.

He discovered they were devout Catholics, rather conservative in their beliefs. Yet it seemed they were trying to project a vastly different image of themselves as super-professional psychologists with ultra-open minds. They seemed determined to set themselves apart from others in their profession; this they did by claiming that they were a cut above their colleagues. The two mindsets did not synchronise well in Peter's eyes. There was an arrogance about their behaviour as they marketed themselves as the best. Peter felt unhappy that Amelia supported them in their claims, without question.

It was the day that the family invited all their kith and kin to dinner, especially to meet Peter, that had made him feel particularly anxious. That's when he sensed that Amelia did not feel altogether comfortable being next to him. They belonged to two different worlds and nothing was going to change that; it stood out a mile.

She was not the same after that and shortly after his departure to Fiji, he received a letter from her ending their relationship. How he wished he had never accepted her parents' invitation. It had been so naïve of him to think that Amelia and he could have had a life together. Peter kept chastising himself for accepting that disastrous invitation. Meeting Amelia's family and friends had highlighted the enduring and unchangeable aspects of culture. They had both felt a sense of stagnation, an inability to address the issues at hand.

For him, the sense of loss had become too onerous to bear. Peter came from a culture where a relationship once formed, endured until death. In his culture, an invitation to spend time in the home of a prospective partner was as good as sealing a marriage contract. The break-up after accepting that invitation to visit was too shameful a burden for him.

The afternoon that he received Amelia's letter, Peter packed a small bag of essentials and left his family home. A brief note to his family informed them to not expect him back; this, together with Amelia's letter to him, he left on the small dining table. Peter no longer cared to be called by his Christian name. He reverted to Banda and disappeared into the wilderness of the Fijian jungle.

*

The room was cramped and dark, there was a strong and pervasive musty aura around; it could have been the papers lying on the floor, but the clothes hanging on the bedstead were musty as well. This was Banda's room and Banda was lying on a rickety makeshift bed which was propped up against a thatched wall. A brick under one leg gave the bed a degree of stability. Banda's body was burning with a fever so terrible that at times he hardly knew who he was or whether he was still alive. It was malaria. He had first caught it during his youth, that once wonderful and fairytale-like time of his life. Wracked with pain, the bouts of consciousness took him on fleeting journeys to that past, to the love of his life, Amelia. He could see her now, just as she had been then, her skin glowing softly, a shimmering white, so stark against his now weathered body which was as black as the night sky. Her hair shone with a radiance that was both red and orange, and when it caught the light of the sun, it shimmered in a myriad of hues. He loved her so much; they had loved each other so much, but then one day, she simply told him that there was no future in this love of theirs. It had to cease immediately.

The shock had been too much for Banda; he had run deep into the Fijian forest, far deeper than he had ever been before. He had meant to end his life, but destiny had somehow intervened and prevented that. For months he had wandered around in the forest, eating little to nothing, crying to the gods to end his life. And then came the recurring bouts of malaria. He had thought it to be the end, but somehow, he had recovered. Discovered by Tikka, the hag, an old woman who seemed as ancient as the forest itself, he had been dragged to shelter and cared for by her over many months.

Banda could see rays of light penetrating the wooden shack that was now home to him; it was daylight once again. He had perspired profusely during the night, turning this way and that, feeling pain in every part of his body. This was Tikka's old home and Banda remembered how, years ago, she had given up this very bed for him when he had first come down with malaria in the forest. He laboured to get up and drink some water from the makeshift water tank which collected the water from the roof. Banda knew it was not safe, but there was no strength left in his body to attempt boiling it. He wiped himself as best as he could and tried to stay upright, shuffling this way and that, but the shivering and shaking would not stop and, eventually, he fell back into the bed with exhaustion. And then he was with Amelia once again.

The many years in the forest had afforded Banda all the time he needed to think. Amelia and he had been too young to even consider marriage. Had he not made that trip with Amelia, their affection for each other would eventually have petered out. It was the invitation from her parents that had been suggestive of a long-term commitment, a commitment that could never be realised. Amelia had been so proud of her parents, that they were psychologists, that they knew so much about human behaviour, that they were worldly wise, yet they knew nothing of his culture or any culture bar their own. How ignorant they had been to experiment with his life! Slowly but surely, he assessed the actions he had taken during that time. Had he been too rash to run away as he had done? Too extreme and harsh on himself? Yes, this was undoubtedly not the best way to spend the rest of his life. He resolved to make amends with himself, more to undo the wrong and hurt he had inflicted on his family, but he needed to get better first.

The monsoon season ended and shortly thereafter, Banda felt well enough to travel. His mind was made up. He would leave his forest dwelling and return to his village. It was a day's walk to the edge of the forest. Banda felt elated, despite not knowing what to expect. He walked along a narrow footpath that took him into the village. How different everything looked. There were so many houses that he did not recognise, but he could see the schoolhouse in the distance. It was confirmation that he was where he should be. It was the beacon that guided him into the loving arms of his mother. The reunion was ecstatic, yet so tearful, but how pleased they both were to hold each other once again.

'Banda, my dear son, how could I be any happier than this? To know that you are here and alive is all that I could wish for until my dying day.'

The tears streamed down both their faces.

She held his face in both her hands, then wiped the tears away from his face. 'Will you forgive me, Banda? This was all my fault. If I had not pushed you to go to Australia, none of this would have happened.' Banda's mother had never ceased to castigate herself for making that foolish mistake.

'Mother, it was not your fault. No, never. It was fate that drove us to do what we did, and we all paid the price for it. But now…now it's behind us, it's over, I hope, and perhaps we can start to live the way we did once again. Come, let us go home. I can't wait to see my sisters. They must be so grown-up now. Tell me all about them and what has happened these last few years,' he said as he gently led her out of the schoolhouse.

The family was overjoyed at Banda's return and they soon organised a reunion to celebrate this long-awaited event. The family had grown. Banda now had two nephews and a niece to get acquainted with. While Banda's mother focused on encouraging him to rest, Banda was already making plans to help his father out as he had always done.

It was a week after he'd returned home that his mother handed Banda a letter that had arrived six months ago. It was from Amelia. She inquired after him and hoped that he was well and happy. She was now married and expressed a hope that one day, she and her husband might visit Fiji and catch up with him and all her friends there. The tone was sincere and honest. Banda was glad to know that Amelia was happy. He felt no bitterness towards her, but meeting her again was not something he felt ready for quite yet. Perhaps time would heal the wounds. Right now, all he wanted was to catch up on all he had missed of his own family, especially the new members. Banda was smiling once again.

A Rollercoaster Ride

The family was excited. We would be hosting a homestay who was Swiss-French, our first from the southern part of Switzerland. Over the years, we had enjoyed the company of many a Swiss-German. Their behaviour was always exemplary; it was their dogmatic concern about time-keeping that amused us no end. What did it matter if the bus was half a minute late? Such things mattered inordinately to most of them. We expected our Swiss-French visitor to provide us with a more relaxed and fluid experience.

Welcome to Brisbane

Answering the doorbell took us all by surprise. Looking very much the part of a male model stood Etienne, our guest to be for the next three months; he was dressed in skin-tight black jeans, a black leather jacket, and boots. He was twenty-three and oozed youthfulness and energy. The icy blue eyes and styled blond hair contrasted sharply with his clothing. Cologne effused from every part of his body, leaving little doubt that he spent a small fortune on his coiffeur. The greeting was flamboyant; the French way with many *allo*s and kisses all round, something my husband Robert loathed and twelve-year-old Jeremy shied away from, but it did break the barriers. And then we were faced with the stark reality that Etienne spoke almost no English, so sign language became the temporary norm. Still, with his unrelenting desire to learn English, he improved in leaps and bounds.

Etienne was overwhelmed with the tropical paradise that was Brisbane; it delighted him no end. He tried tirelessly to tell us how amazed he was at the beautiful stretch of river that he was driven past on his way to us. I could relate to his feeling; the river along Breakfast Creek was always such a deep sky-blue – it never failed to give me the feeling of space and freedom. A brief excursion through the garden became a walk of discovery for Etienne. That we could actually have guavas, passion fruit, mulberries, mangoes and avocados at arm's length and ready for the picking proved difficult for him to take in within such a short space of time.

I took Etienne to his English language school on his first day and gave him instructions on how to return home. When he returned, we were dismayed to find him in a foul mood.

'There is no fucking student I can talk with, not one fucking European at the school. They have students from all countries, from Japan, Korea, Indonesia, Brazil, and Argentina. But not even one who can speak French! I will have no fucking friends to go to the pub with,' moaned Etienne.

Etienne was furiously unhappy. His mother tongue was sacrosanct to him and, with no French speakers in sight, he felt insecure and utterly lost. We clarified Australia's geographical position to him, its proximity to the East. French students coming over here were few and far between. Having no further solution to offer him, we urged him to speak with the principal and make his feelings known. We hoped that yet another explanation might subdue him. This he did, as he told us later with the use of just about every four-letter word in the dictionary. By the third day, and after several ugly battles with the principal, Etienne decided to leave the school. The parting was physical and ugly; it surprised us they had not called the police in, that he wasn't spending a night or two in the lock-up.

Stunned with this dramatic beginning to what should have been his three months of English study in Brisbane, the question remained. 'What next?'

'No problem,' said Etienne. 'I fucking learn English myself. I talk to you… I talk to people in street… I go to backpackers and meet many people there… I don't need no fucking school to learn English,' he said with emphatic and flourishing sweeps of his arms.

The events thus far sparked several calls between Etienne and his parents. Voices were raised to such a crescendo that we could hear both parties speak from the adjacent room. The parents wished him to go back to the school, apologise for his behaviour, carry on with his study, but Etienne was unyielding.

Across the Tasman

We soon learnt that Etienne's potential for landing a good desk job was almost non-existent; he had not finished his schooling. His parents had reckoned that sending him to Australia would give him a fresh start. He could learn English and thereafter spend a year in New Zealand. Family friends in New Zealand owned a large sheep farm where Etienne was to work until he found his feet. His parents tried for weeks to reason with him about the English school, but Etienne stood his ground.

Etienne idled his days away, chatting to backpackers, who seemed to have cast some sort of magical spell on him, and drinking at various pubs. He'd return home for dinner in a vibrant mood with two bottles of wine and a six-pack of beer which he wished to share with us, to drink the night away. In fact, his desire for constant social interaction was draining the little energy we had left after a hard day's work. Thus, his premature departure to New Zealand was an absolute relief to all of us. We quickly slipped back into our comfortable routines. Dinner times now consisted of much talk about what Etienne might be doing in New Zealand. He had created chaos in Brisbane. There was no reason why he wouldn't do the same in New Zealand. We, however, could now do what we wanted in the evenings, such as watch TV, or read a newspaper in quiet. It was a bliss that we had taken for granted in the past.

Back to Oz

I was cooking one morning before going to work when the phone rang.

'Hello, Cathy, it's me, Etienne. What are you doing now?'

'Etienne! How nice to hear from you? How is your job in New Zealand?' I questioned, rather pleased to hear from him.

'New Zealand, I hate New Zealand. I work fifteen hours a day and all I see are sheep, sheep and sheep. There is no one I can talk to and nothing to see but sheep. I hate this bloody job. For fifteen hours a day, I am cutting the tail of the sheep off. Fucking job…fucking New Zealand.'

I was filled with unease; this was not right. It was exactly two weeks since Etienne had left Brisbane.

'Etienne, where are you calling from?' I asked, feeling anxious about what he was going to say.

'I'm here.' said Etienne, in a tone that sounded happy and exhilarated.

'What do you mean by here?' By now, I was beginning to feel a bit panicky.

'Brisbane, I'm in Brisbane,' said Etienne, sounding happy. 'I love Brisbane. Can you pick me up?'

'Etienne, when did you get to Brisbane? And where shall I pick you up? What about your job in New Zealand?' I was thinking of his parents as I asked him this final question. They had gone to great pains to try and turn him into a responsible adult, and with no positive results, it seemed.

'Fuck the job and fuck New Zealand,' said Etienne. 'I got here last night, but I broke my leg and can't walk… I will tell you later, anyway. Can you pick me up? I will be at the backpackers at South Bank. And can you bring some money, about fifty dollars to pay the backpackers? I'll pay you back later.'

'Fine, I'll be there. Just give me about twenty minutes.' My mind was muddled. Etienne was supposed to work on his parents' friends' farm for one year. What on earth would they think of him packing his bags and leaving after just two weeks! What distress and embarrassment for his parents! My mind was full of all these thoughts as I dressed and drove off to pick him up.

I found him seated on the pavement, leaning on his backpack. There was dried mud on his clothes and face, and to all appearances, he looked like a tramp. He had hurt his leg, and I had to help him into the front seat; he winced as he tried to get into a comfortable position.

'What actually happened?' I asked him, not knowing where I wished him to start his story. 'How did your break your leg?'

'I fell from a tree,' said Etienne.

'You fell out of a tree! Can you explain, please?'

'It's a long story. I was in the botanical garden. I climbed a tree, but I fell, and when I tried to get up, I couldn't, so I think I must have broken something, my knee, I think. It was about two in the morning and I couldn't see anything. I was shouting for help, but there was no one around. Finally, a man heard me and he helped me to the backpackers.'

I was driving while listening to this eventful and rather pitiful tale. 'I suppose you'd drunk a fair bit by then,' I said, trying to make it sound as casual as possible.

'Well, I had one or two drinks at the pub with some friends I met... You know, Cathy, it's so great to be back in Brisbane... I was so happy I wanted to celebrate. The people here are so great, so I had a few drinks with my friends, and then I went and did this shit thing! Fucking shit! I guess I'll have to go to the hospital. It's not the first time I have broken my knee.'

I was slowly getting the picture. Having one or two drinks with friends would merely translate into drinking till he was blotto. Etienne would have been paying for drinks all round, his usual style of trying to be the centrepiece. As soon as the cash ran out, the so-called friends would have disappeared, leaving Etienne to his own devices. Undeterred, he had made his way to the botanical garden, perhaps hoping for an audience among the homeless. Climbing the tree may have been his way of entertaining them, or perhaps it was just a case of entertaining himself. The latter seemed more likely, as he said there was no one to help him when he found that he could not move. He had shouted for help and finally dozed off, or passed out. Eventually, a good Samaritan turned up and helped him to the backpackers for the night.

I had to settle the bill at the backpackers; Etienne's wallet had been well and truly emptied. How sad, I thought, that this twenty-three-year-old had travelled halfway around the world, and yet could not differentiate between friend and exploiter. He was undermining the goodwill of his parents to buy friends; it seemed to be the only thing that made him feel secure. I took him home and made him comfortable. He was grateful for that; home comforts were important to him.

Etienne needed surgery and our GP booked him into hospital. So yet another day was tied up with transporting him to and from the hospital. The house was in chaos with Etienne's constant ranting and barbaric use of the English language. He had little vocabulary for polite conversation but for anything verging on rudeness, his supply of four-letter words seemed endless. It left little space for normal conversation. He could not be quiet for a moment, yet had nothing of consequence or interest to say. The strain on the family was immense.

Homeward bound to Lausanne

After his convalescence with us, Etienne moved to the backpackers, that magical world that attracted him, in search of 'friends' who would willingly drink with him and listen to his stories. Yet, like a homing pigeon, he never failed to visit us three or four times a week with two bottles of wine and a six-pack tucked under his arm. Etienne had developed a certain rapport with Megan, our daughter, and was always keen to find out what she had done at school with her friends. He was with us when we celebrated Megan's birthday in mid-April, and was thrilled to bits organising games for her friends. It was heart-warming to see the sincerity with which he took part in her birthday activities.

Being so much a part of the family, it appeared Etienne would never leave. When he finally decided to return to Switzerland, it was after near on seven months of idleness in Brisbane. It was October, and the landscape was dotted with the beautiful lavender blossoms of the jacaranda trees. Now devoid of foliage but covered with the blooms, it turned entire avenues into purple pathways.

The drive to the airport was spectacular and magical, a mood that did not reflect Etienne's feelings about his departure.

*

Over the next three years, Etienne returned to Brisbane five times, staying with us a few nights each time, then moving to the backpackers for the rest of his stay. His interests had not changed; he needed lots of 'friends' to drink with and cheer him on, and he was willing to empty his wallet to that end. He had as yet never held down a job, so it was his parents' money that he was throwing away so freely, and on people he would possibly never see again.

I believe Etienne almost felt that we were his family. Over the years, he always gave us the occasional call from Switzerland and I was much surprised when he communicated to me that he was working in a high managerial position at the local agricultural cooperative close to Lausanne. He had much to boast about, and rightly so, I thought on that occasion. I was planning a trip to Europe at that time to visit family in Switzerland, and I felt it would be nice to meet Etienne's family while I was there. Etienne was overjoyed, and with his usual generosity, insisted that I stay a week with his family. I expected to meet a very changed Etienne. He was twenty-nine, and I felt confident that with the job he now held, and the six years that had elapsed, he would have crossed the threshold into adulthood.

The hospitality extended by his family overwhelmed me. They had planned an excursion for each day of my visit, something I had not expected. Etienne talked non-stop as usual; his English had improved immensely. It was winter and Etienne drove me across the mountains to several smallholding wineries; we enjoyed boutique brews with local cheese, and air-dried meats from the Wallis region. He then started telling me about his hugely important job (his father, through his influence, had unwisely secured this position for him). He, Etienne, was preparing to deliver a seminar to two hundred managers... I could hardly believe it, given the population figures of the area. Etienne was merely being boastful, trying to impress me with his importance.

Post-event saw a very deflated Etienne; only one person had turned up, to his great disappointment. I tried to give him some advice about managing people and events, but doubt that he took anything of what I said to heart. Six years had passed, and it seemed as though Etienne had changed very little.

It broke my heart when his mother approached me for help with her hapless son. She felt that I was the only person able to connect with Etienne, able to give him some advice; such a never-ending saga of undesirable events. She was concerned about his involvement with a Russian girl. 'Mafia connections,' she remarked.

The fact was that no decent girl was willing to enter into a relationship with Etienne. He remained too defiant, rude, arrogant and egotistic. He was also intensely jealous of his two siblings, both academically astute and well settled in life. Sadly, it had polarised the family, and I believe Etienne felt singled out as the black sheep.

The Russian girlfriend was a tough call for me to address but I soon found out that Etienne was in absolutely no hurry to get married; it was, however, very much what the girlfriend wanted. The undesirable relationship had prompted his father to discontinue his allowance, and living within his means was not proving to be particularly easy. It also meant that Etienne was now under pressure to hold down his job, whether he liked it or not. His earnings could not support him plus another. More to the point, his earnings did not allow him to have the riotous life that he wished to lead. Having to support himself had subdued him, made him more responsible.

*

Two years on, a call from Etienne confirmed that he had indeed changed. He had married the Russian girl, perhaps simply because all his friends were now married. While he did not appear to be excited about married life, it was not the disaster his parents thought it would be; on the contrary, it was the making of Etienne. No doubt under his wife's guidance, Etienne was now enrolled in a business school, diligently studying to improve his career prospects. He had changed his job. Now employed in the postal service, he could, through perseverance and study, be able to further himself. He was finally in a position to be the master of his destiny. Speaking to his wife on the phone gave me a clear impression that she had the strength and patience to guide Etienne towards success; she was the best thing that had happened to Etienne. His journey into adulthood had finally begun.

Kev, Gus, and a Lot of Fuss

Kevin was more cheerful than usual as he stepped out of the front door; having bade farewell to his wife, he headed briskly on foot to work. It was the beginning of a new academic year, and he had a lot to be grateful for. He had not been one of the many redundancies of the university and had just returned from a three-week stint in Vietnam, enjoying the sun and the food that he loved. He'd been trying to build a network of small to medium-sized businesses in Asia, a proposition that he'd pitched to the university. Kevin was passionate about the East but sadly he felt that the risk-averse British managers at the university did not share his enthusiasm.

Kevin's major weakness was his blind faith that he could make anyone a millionaire overnight. His endless list of 'get rich quick' plans were always well subscribed to but delivered nothing. It agitated people to no end. Threatening letters and physical encounters became the norm. Thus, acquaintances disappeared as quickly as he acquired them and friends were few and far between.

And so it was that when Kevin became a household name in his youthful years in England, and for the wrong reasons, he packed his bags and sought his fortunes in Germany. Germany was much harder to tackle, so Kevin had to take on a dead-end job and work for his crust. That was no way to live, but wait a minute, every cloud has a silver lining, even though that cloud may be on the far and distant horizon. Kevin was packing his bags again; this time, he proudly sported the badge of 'Ten Pound Pom' as he departed Southampton, England, for Sydney in Down Under, Australia.

It was the best thing that could have happened to him. Things went pretty well out there; he produced a myriad of business ideas and made a sound living selling hope to the gullible and worked his way through Melbourne, Adelaide and Perth, eventually arriving in Brisbane. That's when the silver on the cloud seemed to tarnish. His business ideas had lost their lustre; they did not evoke so much as a whisper of the enthusiasm he'd expected.

Kevin wondered whether he'd lost his touch, but dismissed that immediately. 'Impossible!' he said. 'It's the credit crunch and the crash of the euro. What a bother. I'll just have to work a bit harder.'

'Kevin, the world is changing. People are thinking hard and fast about their cash,' remarked the voice of his invisible friend. 'There are no millions in store for you, my friend. Get a proper job, get a proper job, get a proper job.' The voice kept on and on.

Eventually, Kevin listened; he packed his bags and returned to his homeland with his second wife and young family.

Throughout his colourful life and before his second marriage, Kevin had learned one useful lesson; image was of utmost importance. To sell himself and his ideas, he needed to project the image of a resilient and experienced world-class manager. Appearance and talk had to complement each other. Kevin had become a master of disguise.

With the assistance of a friend, he sold himself as a business entrepreneur and secured a tutoring position at a London university. It was stable and secure, but so terribly sedate for Kevin. He had worked for the university for less than a year when it dawned on him that he could use his business acumen to expand the operations of the university into Asia. Asia was the new oasis, and Vietnam the land of milk and honey. Kevin recalled the meeting of departmental heads he had organised before the summer, to share his business idea; the frosty reception he had received had made him feel like knocking a few heads together; and had it not been for that invisible angel over his shoulder saying, 'Kevin, take it easy, keep your cool,' he very nearly might have done so.

That was then, before his business trip. Right now, he was armed with a list of Vietnamese businesses interested in his offer. He had typed part of the report, and he planned on spending the day tidying it up. Life felt good, and Kevin was more than pleased as he sprinted up to his office door that autumn morning.

It was only on turning the key that Kevin remembered that his co-occupant, Janet, would soon be moving out together with her six boxes. University space came at a premium so every box was regarded as an invasion of the much-desired commodity of space. He looked forward to the departure of the six boxes. His new office mate was going to be Gustav Fischer. Gus was generally known as the pedantic German who was always right; pretty much everyone described him as a bore. Kevin had heard the gossip but, having never met Gus, he was willing to give the man a chance. That was until he entered the room and found that Janet had already moved out and Gus had moved in. The scene confronting him left him in a profound state of shock; Gus had taken seventy-five per cent of the room and rammed Kevin's desk behind the door. While surveying this disaster, the man himself appeared.

'Hmm, so I must share with you,' he said with his strong Bavarian accent. 'I like my desk to face the room, not the wall.'

'It is a very small room and Janet and I had worked out what we felt was the best use for this small space. Don't you think we should discuss…' but Kevin was stopped short.

'I like the room like this,' said Gus and with that, he turned on his heel and left.

'So much for cordial relations!' thought Kevin.

The malicious streak in Kevin was already in charge. Kevin was blessed with a vivid imagination and a good sense of humour; it often led people to misread his true nature. His departmental heads had worked this out and knew him for what he was; hence their constant rebuttal of all his fantastic ideas, which were more than often based on whimsical dreams rather than sound research.

Poor Gus was ignorant of Kevin's capacity to be vindictive; he did not know what was to come. And now that Gus was proving to be uncooperative, he, Kevin, was going to create no end of havoc for him.

Leaving his briefcase aside, Kevin took off his jacket, rolled up his sleeves and moved everything back as it had been with Janet. Pleased with the outcome, Kevin got down to his paperwork. But being fired up with the morning's unpleasantness, he was itching to see Gus's reaction to the rearrangement; it was profoundly difficult for him to concentrate on work. Kevin did not know if Gus would return that day or not, but every time he heard footsteps along the corridor, he pretended to be busy and prepared himself for a verbal offensive.

There were footsteps again. 'It's him, get ready, it's him,' said Kevin's trusted little voice. 'Thanks for that, chum,' said Kevin, as he prepared for the onslaught.

Kevin composed himself as the approaching footsteps got louder and louder before stopping outside the office door. The door was slightly ajar and the sturdy push banged it against the wall. Gus's jaw dropped and his mouth fell open in a look worthy of a photo. He had not in a million years expected the room to be rearranged as before. His face changed colour from white to pink to red and redder.

'But I don't want my' (Kevin was quick to note it was not 'our') 'office to look like this. I don't want my chair facing the wall. I want my chair to face the room so that I can see my students. And I don't...'

Kevin interrupted, 'Well, I would like my chair facing the room as well, but as you can see, this is a tiny room. Personally, I have no problem with you having your chair facing the room as long as there is enough room for my desk to have a reasonable position.'

Kevin outwardly maintained calm, but still fumed at the fact that Gus had no intention of being amiable. Retribution was the word Kevin had for what was going on. It was a word his mother had often used, and it had stuck. Gus was the wrongdoer and Kevin was merely putting him in his place, making him see the wrongness of his actions. That it afforded Kevin an immense amount of pleasure was beside the point.

Gus huffed and puffed and waited for his blood pressure to drop before gathering his belongings and leaving the office. He was not used to people challenging him in this manner. 'How dare they, they had no right to, these English, they needed putting in their places,' he thought as he struggled to decide on his next move. That would have to wait. At the moment, he was in no state to challenge this lunatic, but tomorrow would see a stronger and more able Gus.

Kevin sat back in his chair and turned on his radio; the music soothed him, helped him to compose himself. Kevin had developed a need for greatness during his early years in England. His had been an impoverished and deprived life. With no paternal control in the home, he had always slipped past his mother with the ease of an eel. His time was more than often spent with the wrong sort of people, the sort who exploited the weakness of others for their personal benefit. He was dazzled by them, at the ease with which they flashed ill-gained profits around. They made life seem so terribly easy. He remembered Andy boasting about the way he would have it off with the ladies and then have them hand over their cash. Kevin had learned to expect great things without necessarily having to work for his reward.

Kevin did not get back to his office until Tuesday afternoon; he was not surprised to find that Gus had moved things back to how he wanted them. This was definitely not a good start for the year. 'Kick-up-a-fuss-Gus' had not learnt his lesson. He was not going to cooperate, and Kevin was not going to stand for that.

Rolling up his shirt sleeves, he manoeuvred Gus's desk into a corner. This did allow Gus to have his chair facing the room, as he so adamantly wished. Kevin then moved his coffee table next to Gus's desk. 'Yes, that does look good,' thought Kevin, as he broke out into hoots of laughter. The only way that Gus could get to his chair was by jumping over his desk. Kevin was still shaking with laughter when Gus turned up.

'What have you done to my desk?' queried Gus, looking thoroughly outraged. 'I can't even get to my chair,' he complained with a moan. 'Why do we need to have this table here? Can't it go somewhere else?'

'Oh, I suppose we could put it somewhere else. I'll see to it,' chimed Kevin in a cheerful voice. 'I think this is a much better arrangement though, don't you? And your chair is facing the room as you wanted it to.'

There was no reply from Gus, just a horribly disgusting look that did his austere appearance no good. As for Kevin, well, he was as happy as a lark and whistled his favourite tune 'These boots are made for walking' as he made his way home that evening.

'You seem to be in a good mood,' said Julie, his wife.

'Yes, it's been a pretty good day.'

'Have you finished that report then?'

'It's almost ready,' replied Kevin.

In truth, he had not so much as looked at it over the past few days. Besides, he was not yet finished with Gus. Kevin emptied the brass-handled chest of drawers that he had by his bedside; he had acquired it a few weeks ago at the Portobello market.

The next morning saw Kevin lugging the chest of drawers on his trolley wheels to his office. He was puffing by the time he got the damn thing there; the chest of drawers kept insisting on falling over sideways. He made a quick mental note to complain to the council about the potholes on the pavement, then heaved a sigh of relief at seeing his office door. Now he could get down to business. Gus had complained about the coffee table, so Kevin replaced it with the chest of drawers. He then emptied his kettle and placed it inside the drawer together with his mug, tea, coffee and a packet of digestives. Gus wanted the coffee table removed, which Kevin had done, and scored another point as a bonus.

When Gus arrived, he was silent for a moment. 'Why do we need this thing here?' he cried out. He appeared to be breaking into a sweat.

Kevin looked innocently at him with a questioning look on his face. 'But where do you expect me to keep my kettle and tea and coffee? You didn't want the coffee table, so I brought this for my things,' retorted Kevin, as he opened the drawers to show Gus the contents.

Gus was nearly shaking, but he was too angry to say anything. Without another word, he squeezed past the chest of drawers to his chair. With a weary look, he sat down, heaved a sigh and buried his face in his work.

Kevin put his time into dreaming up more schemes for becoming a millionaire. The problem with Kevin's schemes was that they lacked sound foundations, they were based purely on his impressive imagination and the ability to persuade others to jump on board with the cash. When one scheme crashed, he would come up with another almost instantaneously, but the burnt prospectors had by then disappeared.

It took a lot to dampen Kevin's spirits and, as always, he would say, 'I had the simplest and most fantastic business proposition for all of us to make a lot of money with just a small investment, but the English/Germans/Australians are far too short-sighted to see the benefits of my scheme. I honestly don't know how they end up becoming managers when they can't see a good thing coming. Even after having showed them all the figures of my pilot study, which I undertook at my own expense, all they could do was um and ah. If only they had just tried it, we could all by now be sitting pretty as millionaires.'

A day and a half passed in the shared office with barely a word said between the two. The atmosphere was sour, not what Kevin wanted. With two people in such a small room, the air was getting stuffy.

Gus was finding it difficult to cope with the stale air. 'Is there no ventilation in this room?'

Kevin was quick off the mark. 'Why don't you open the window if it's bothering you?'

And so it was that Gus squeezed out of his cramped corner and went over to the window. He undid the latches, which seemed stuck fast, and then, with both hands firmly on the handles, he lifted the window. It did lift, but to his utter surprise the entire window came off and he fell backwards with it. Poor Gus looked a sorry state as he lay on the floor under a large sash window that was pinning him down. Kevin had known precisely what to expect; the window had broken last year and had not been fixed as yet.

'Now look what you've done,' said Kevin, as he helped Gus to his feet. 'And winter's on its way. Just look at that bleak, slate-grey sky outside. We're going to be freezing in here with no window. I think you'll have to call the maintenance people to have it fixed,' said Kevin, feeling completely smug about the whole affair. And then he heard that little voice.

'You'll never get to heaven like this, Kevin. Shouldn't you be a little nicer to him?' But Kevin replied with a silent 'Oh, shut up for now, will ya' as he dusted his trousers down and gave himself another score in his little red book.

It was a good end to the week. Kevin gathered up his belongings and went home, feeling pleased with having taught Gus yet another lesson. Hopefully, the window would be fixed over the weekend. He would soon have Gus eating out of his hand and enjoying it. But now it was time for the family, and this weekend they had planned a trip to the Isle of Wight to enjoy each other's company. It would give Kevin the time he needed to plan his week.

Sunday evening made him realise that he had done almost none of the work that should have been completed last week. He would need to work hard to get back on schedule. Once again, he was going to have to rely on delay tactics and petty fibs, exaggerations and his ability to sell dreams. It was, as always, a case of overestimation of self and underestimation of others. With due credit, Kevin's optimism was undaunting. It had to be; after all, he had managed to convince his wife about the feasibility of the current project and had spent all their savings on his 'business trip' to Vietnam.

As Kevin unlocked the office door that Monday morning, he was expecting to see a brand-new window in the office and there certainly was one, but that was not what caught his attention. Sitting in the middle of the room and blocking his view of the window were nine big tea chests, Gus's boxes. Janet's six boxes had been too much to cope with and he had been glad to see them go, but now there were nine.

This really was too much. It was time to roll up his sleeves once again. Kevin moved the boxes, carefully stacking them in front of Gus's desk. And just to be nice, he left a small space in the middle, too tight a space for a chair, so that Gus had a tightly tunnelled view. And then

Kevin sat down to his work, the work which should have been done last week.

It was not long before Gus arrived, accompanied by a student. He was taken aback by what confronted him.

'Morning, Gus. Did you have a pleasant weekend?' said Kevin, without looking up and giving the impression of being terribly busy.

'Yes, yes, fine,' replied Gus. Then turning to his student, he said, 'I have to get things sorted out here, so perhaps we'd better go to the library for now.'

Gus returned about an hour later without his student. He moved silently like a ghost and having got successfully past the obstacle course; he managed to sidle into his chair. Then, setting up his laptop, he immersed himself in his work.

'I really can't understand why you have so much stuff,' said Kevin. 'Janet had six boxes, and we had a problem accommodating them. But you've got even more. Nine boxes! I can't believe it,' remarked Kevin. I don't have any boxes and just as well.' remarked Kevin, without looking up.

There was no return comment from Gus, who appeared to have thrown himself, heart and soul, into his work.

At about three in the afternoon, Gus received a phone call, which he answered in hushed tones. It sounded like something urgent. He quickly stuffed the sausage roll that he had bought for lunch into his mouth and rushed off in a great hurry. Kevin lay back in his chair, feeling relaxed at last.

'What a bugger,' thought Kevin and then his eyes began to twinkle. An opportunity was smiling at him once again. Kevin quickly closed the office door and then squeezed up to Gus's desk. Grabbing the keyboard, which he had recognised to be a wireless one, he turned it over and removed the batteries. There was no time to hang around now. He stuffed his belongings into his briefcase, left the office unlocked and went home in a noticeable hurry.

Kevin did not consider himself mean in any way, but he did enjoy a good practical joke; more to the point, he revelled in them. It was never in his nature to be wilfully destructive, but he found annoying people to be of immense fun. That was usually the outcome when he found the other party uncompromising and resistant to accepting necessary change. Gus was sadly not one who was willing to share space with anyone, nor was he one to enjoy a good joke or have a friendly laugh. Kevin knew that this would not be a good year unless he managed to annoy Gus to the point where he would not spend much time in the office. Managing Gus was turning out to be quite a job.

Kevin forgot all about the batteries until the next morning as he strode briskly to work. There was a crisp chill in the air and the mist was only just rising; he did not like the cold and a sudden shudder went through his spine. How he wished he could be back in Vietnam. Hopefully, his business plan would be approved and that would mean that he could spend most of the academic year in the sun, divided equally between Vietnam and his adopted home, Australia. He would faithfully devote this day to finishing his report. Thursday afternoon had been set aside for the presentation that he hoped would make others finally see the light. Thereafter, he hoped it would be plain sailing; such was his optimism. He chuckled to himself on remembering the batteries and tried to imagine Gus's face, seething with anger and getting all worked up.

Kevin entered the office and noticed a large piece of cardboard on his desk. Written on it with a red marker was Gus's accusation: 'I know you stole my batteries, YOU THIEF.'

This was far worse, much worse than Kevin had ever expected. How utterly despicable of Gus to accuse him (Kevin) of an offence that he had not witnessed. Gus's inability to get on with people was far worse than Kevin had imagined. He would need to speak to Gus and sort this out once and for all, if that was possible, of course. In the meantime, Kevin needed to safeguard his sanctity. He sat down at his desk, toying with the piece of cardboard as he thought of his next step. His mind lit up.

Leaving his briefcase in the office, he donned his jacket and scarf and hurried off towards the main street and the shops. His destination was Woolworths and there he bought a pack of batteries, the cheapest of course, that would fit Gus's keyboard. He was in a hurry, preferring to get back before Gus arrived at the office. Gus had not arrived, and that gave Kevin time to compose himself and place the batteries on Gus's desk. Then, sitting at his own desk, he went through different scenarios of how he was going to react towards Gus and what they would say to each other. 'What a bother,' thought Kevin, 'the poor sod can't take anything as a joke.' Kevin settled down to work on his report, and the day passed without further incident. Gus did not turn up that day.

Wednesday turned out to be another chilly day with gusty winds. Kevin was glad to get into his office and settle down to work while dreaming of a life in sunny climes. Kevin never dabbled in anything modest; that was for the small fry. His was always a multimillion-dollar scheme where he would reap his millions within a short period of one or two years at the most. His very trusting wife was soon swept off her feet with the prospect of such riches; little did she know of Kevin's numerous such schemes before their marriage, schemes that had on each occasion left him near destitute. But Kevin had that remarkable capacity to always re-emerge, with just a few minor scratches and bruises to his ego.

The sound of footsteps alerted him to Gus's arrival.

'Good morning, Gus,' said Kevin in a slightly severe tone of aloofness.

'How dare you steal my batteries?' blurted Gus angrily.

'And how dare you accuse me of stealing your batteries? Did you see me steal them? Did you?' asked Kevin. 'And if I did steal them, why would I bother to go and get you a new set of batteries? If I had really stolen your batteries, I would simply give you back your old batteries. But as you have accused me of stealing something, which I haven't, I have gone and bought you a new set of batteries with my own money simply to keep you happy. Don't you think that anyone could have come into the office while the door was open?' Kevin knew that he had Gus cornered.

Gus remained quiet for a while, simply turning over the pack of batteries in his hand. 'I think I might have got this wrong, I'm sorry,' said Gus, looking rather sheepish and not enjoying it in the least.

'Shall we just put this behind us then and try to get along a bit better?' asked Kevin, seeing this as an opportunity for peace and harmony to reign at last. All Kevin wanted was someone nice to share the office with, someone who could enjoy having a laugh and a bit of fun.

'Yes,' said Gus. 'I know we Germans don't have the same way of thinking as you English, but yes, it is important that we try to get on.'

The air cleared a little, and both Kevin and Gus relaxed and sat down to work more productively.

Finally, Kevin felt he could get his report tidied up for his meeting on Thursday. Both worked profusely for about an hour before Kevin felt the need for a cuppa. He got his kettle out of the chest of drawers and made himself a nice cup of Earl Grey tea. Kevin was a tidy person, he never liked leaving a mess; he unplugged the kettle and put it back in the drawer, but on the spur of the moment he deftly removed the adaptor and slipped it into his pocket. The kettle was something that he had purchased while living in Australia, and he was not keen on anyone else using it. But it also went without saying that Kevin always had a trick up his sleeve. His little voice wagged a finger at him, but Kevin cast it aside; just one little game was all he wanted.

Half an hour later, Gus got up and tried to get the kettle boiling for a much-needed drink. He looked puzzled. The plug was definitely not one that would fit a British socket. There had to be a way around, but he was far too proud to ask.

After almost three minutes had elapsed, Kevin chimed in cheerily. 'Are you having a problem with the kettle? Here, let me get it going for you,' he said in a mild tone of feigned kindness.

Unseen by Gus, he whisked the adaptor out of his pocket, fitted it on the plug, and had the kettle going within seconds. 'There you are,' he said to a slightly bewildered Gus, who remained none the wiser about what had happened.

Gus was only too pleased to have a cup of tea, which he now needed even more than before, but that look of confusion on his face each time he used the kettle was there to stay. And each time he did use the kettle, Kevin would nonchalantly chime in, 'Do you need any help with the kettle?' Poor Gus could only feel more and more sheepish about the whole affair. But now it was time for Kevin to do battle with more important people.

Kevin had spent little real time charting out a professional business plan during that week. As usual, he had thrown himself fully into enjoying his childish pranks and, despite the odd hour here and there when he had mostly looked at lists of names and phone contacts, he had not managed to come up with a concrete proposal.

Thursday morning dawned, and Kevin was dressed in his best suit. He had a report of sorts in hand, one that had been produced overnight. With his wife's blessings bestowed on him, he felt that he could confidently gloss over the shortcomings of the report with his verbal defence of Asian business. After all, he had been there in person, and at his own cost. He closed his briefcase, patted it smugly, and set off to meet his colleagues in the office of the vice-chancellor. He approached the last set of traffic lights. They had only just turned red; not wishing to be late for this very important meeting, Kevin decided to chance it. He looked right, then left and made a dash for it.

The motorbike lay overturned in the next lane. Kevin could see the motorcyclist being lifted into the ambulance, and then it was his turn. His entire body was wracking with pain, but he knew he was in expert hands. The paramedics were reassuring him as they lifted him gently but deftly onto the ambulance trolley. He closed his eyes, only to open them very quickly to an extremely disturbing vision. It was Gus, also on his way to the campus. And Gus was holding up his briefcase. It was the briefcase that contained his report.

'Don't worry, Kevin, I'll look after your case for you.' Gus was all smiles.

'Let me have it. I'll take it with me,' said Kevin.

But no one heard those words. The ambulance doors shut just as a shudder of pain made Kevin close his eyes to that million-dollar plan of his.

Miss Pak Goes on Holiday

Miss Pak was a colleague of ours, an English teacher of Korean birth. My husband and I worked at an educational institute located a good four hours south of Seoul by train. The city had a population of two million, with English speakers accounting for but a mere handful. Although in her mid-twenties and unmarried, Miss Pak appeared to have little ambition outside of simply doing the job she had with a mechanical type of dedication. It was the way of life in this part of the world. Life was all about fulfilling the expectations of one's elders and passion did not enter life's equation at any point. So, in that light, one could be tempted to say that she was passionate about her job.

Of all our other colleagues, who numbered around ten, she was perhaps the most personable and did her utmost to help us adjust to our new environment. As most of the teachers at the institute spoke little to no English, Miss Pak took on the role of interpreter and, in addition, she took on the task of explaining the many things that were strange to us. Apart from the fact that she taught English in a didactic and archaic manner, we knew very little about Miss Pak.

It surprised us when one day Miss Pak informed us that she was going on holiday. Taking holidays, we found, was somewhat out of the norm in the Korean workplace and the fact that we had a four-week holiday included in our contract was seen with varying degrees of disdain by our Korean counterparts. While they said nothing explicit to us when we mentioned taking a week off, we did sense a cold aloofness from many of our colleagues; some even made a point of telling us with a degree of pride that Koreans worked hard and did not need holidays. The hint of jealousy about Peter and me having time off was implied without a doubt. Still, there was nothing we could do about the preferential contract we had and possibly even less that they could do about the matter. Had they broached the matter with the owner of the business, a woman as tough as a rhino, they would more than likely have ended up on a permanent holiday.

In any case, we were pleasantly taken aback when Miss Pak told us that she would be going to Seoul for a week and it was for a holiday; she was off to have a good time, though she had asserted firmly to us that she had no family in Seoul. We wished her a happy week and, knowing that this was something out of the ordinary, looked forward to hearing all about it on her return.

Miss Pak's absence was acutely felt by both of us; we had no one else to speak with apart from each other. The Monday of her return soon arrived and Peter and I felt like we were greeting an old friend after a very long absence.

'Good morning, Miss Pak,' said Peter, with a twinkle in his eye and a nod.

'Hello, Miss Pak, how was your holiday? Did you enjoy yourself?' I asked her curiously.

'Good morning,' she said in her staccato voice. 'I enjoyed my holiday in Seoul very much. But I am glad to be back at work. I missed my friends and my students as well.'

'How could you possibly miss this place? You were only away for a week,' said Peter, somewhat surprised by her reply. 'So tell us, what did you get up to over there?'

'Get up to?'

'Sorry, I meant, what did you do in Seoul, what did you go to see, what places did you visit?' clarified Peter.

'Yes, we want to hear all about it,' I said, waiting expectantly. I was particularly curious to know what sort of things Koreans did on holiday.

Peter and I kept looking at Miss Pak and waiting, waiting with curious excitement. Strangely, Miss Pak did much the same; she kept looking at us, her mouth half open, and with a questioning look on her face. It was a bit like *Waiting for Godot*. Neither Peter nor I knew what to make of it. The silence was eventually broken.

'I went to Seoul,' said Miss Pak, in a slightly nervous and faltering voice.

'Yes, Miss Pak, we know you went to Seoul,' said Peter in a gentler tone, assuming that she had not understood the gist of the conversation. 'But what did you do while you were there? Did you go to the theatre, did you visit friends, and did you go shopping?' We both felt that this had clarified the earlier, perhaps hasty words, and smiled to put her at ease. We waited.

'I went to Seoul,' said Miss Pak, yet again with a look of extreme confusion on her face.

Somehow, the conversation seemed to have stalled. She had repeatedly indicated that she had been to Seoul, and that it constituted her holiday; getting past that point seemed quite an impossibility for her, and we were certainly not going to find out what she had done there. I got the definite impression that she thought us to be stupid idiots for not understanding what she had said time and time again to us, the 'ignorant foreigners' as her look suggested.

Peter and I had only about a month before had a brief break in Seoul; we were based in a provincial city about four and a half hours south of Seoul, very much a backwater. It had been fun and exciting to visit Seoul and be back in the realms of a developed city. We had stayed at the Swiss Hotel to have access to some European food and done the usual sightseeing tour of the city: the Olympic Stadium, the leather goods market, bookshops with English-language books (a major highlight for us), and the UPA headquarters, where we had an appointment with a friend in the publishing industry. It had been pleasing to have had access to cafés and restaurants with reasonable toilet facilities, something that our city, Kwang-Ju, certainly lacked. We were also impressed by the variety of international cuisine. Again, something that was unavailable in Kwang-Ju. Without a doubt, Kwang-Ju and Seoul are much like chalk and cheese, so Miss Pak's inability to at least comment on some of the differences seemed decidedly odd to us. She may have gone around with her 'eyes closed' as many people tend to do, but what had she done during the week? Had she spent it reading in a library, had she attended a seminar or conference, or had she simply enjoyed shopping in a proper supermarket? This we would never find out from Miss Pak's lips, and it made me even more curious to find out why she would not, or could not, tell us something which we felt was so blatantly simple.

Peter and I tried to make the most of our long weekends travelling to other cities and towns to explore. Everything was such a world away from home, and trying to make sense of what we saw and experienced was not always easy. Transport, we found, was extremely well organised, providing one could read the signs in Korean. This we could not do, and once again it was Miss Pak who instructed us on which bus or train to take, how long the journey would be and so forth. We found the bus and train stations challenging; they were always packed with people and gave the impression that Koreans were eternally on the move.

The older generations and many of the young as well carried their belongings in bundles of all sizes, which were wrapped and tied with cloth. But the strangest thing of all was the number of people who appeared to be having a rest and were laid out on the station floor upon mats of straw or cloth. There were reclining bodies everywhere, and one had to be careful not to tread on them. They seemed totally at home in this situation, many fast asleep, others eating rice with their many side dishes of meat and vegetable laid out around their patch, and still others simply watching the world go by. When they finished eating, they would neatly stack and wrap up the utensils into a cloth bundle and settle down for a nap. Some even had little oil burners alight to warm their food and surprisingly, the authorities seemed unperturbed about it.

There was little sign of anyone being in a hurry to catch a train or bus. They seemed to be there to stay for a few days at least, with bedding laid out and almost always surrounded by containers of food. I wondered if these were displaced or homeless people but soon dismissed that theory. These individuals were reasonably dressed and had on clean clothes; besides, there were entire families as well with little children running around or playing with their toys and there was no sign of anyone begging. Time and time again, Peter and I experienced this same scene at all the stations we travelled through. These were not transiting passengers as one would expect them to be; there was a feeling of semipermanence about their stay at the station.

It was while I was mesmerised by such a scene one day that I suddenly saw Miss Pak materialise amidst the throng of station residents. No, she was not there; it was just my imagination but here was the answer to the puzzle of Miss Pak's holiday. She certainly had gone to Seoul, and I have no doubt in my mind now that she had spent the week camped out in the station premises like the myriads of other Koreans. No wonder our silly questions confused her!

A Bed of Granite With Satin Sheets

I would never have guessed that behind the façade of quiet tranquillity portrayed by South Koreans, love, lust and betrayal are just as active and alive as in all other societies. Feeling rather uncertain of myself, I made my way towards Ju-Hyun's apartment block. This was a new housing development, mostly finished but, as with most building sites in Korea, the rubble would remain uncleared, an eyesore for near eternity. The night's rain intensified the smells of rotting fish and vegetables, and scantily clad little children played amongst the rubbish heaps. Ju-Hyun's instructions were precise, and I was soon whisked in with a profusion of welcomes by this lithe and energetic young mother of two little children under the age of three.

'Kate, I'm so happy to see you. I didn't think that you would come. Thank you so much for coming to visit me. I want so much for us to be good friends. And I have so much to ask you, I mean about yourself, and also if there is any advice that you can give me… You are older than me and you are not Korean, so you have a lot of experience. I think you could help me a lot…'

It was rather over the top for me from someone who had accosted me at the bus stop a few nights ago and insisted that we could and almost certainly would become friends. She made no secret of the fact that she had been following me for almost a week since first sighting me in her suburb. This came across as blatantly outlandish and bizarre to me, but this was the surprise factor of another culture. Ordinarily, I would have turned down her invitation but to hear the rare sound of English being spoken in this part of the world made me change my mind; I agreed. I had to also come to terms with the fact that the many things I would have considered rude on home soil were evidently not so here. What she had made abundantly clear to me was that she was desperate to talk to someone, someone who was not Korean.

In contrast to the unsavoury flavour of the external environment, the apartment was exceptionally spacious and luxurious. It smelt of money and Ju-Hyun made that explicitly clear to me with pride.

'I would like you to call me Jan… It's the English name they gave me when I worked for the American missionaries. So, what do you think of my apartment? Is it nice? It's very expensive and I am so lucky that my husband is very rich. He's a solicitor. I can buy anything I want, he is so very rich! Shall we have some tea?'

'Well, you're indeed very lucky to have a rich husband and such a beautiful apartment. It looks great…fantastic, I'd say.' I understood clearly that Jan was fishing for compliments.

She was pleased to see me looking around and taking everything in.

We sat down to tea and Jan had certainly done her utmost to prepare a Western-style spread just for me. Her three-year-old was walking on the tabletop we were eating at. To my surprise, Jan did not admonish her, so it was acceptable behaviour. Her other child was under a year old and thankfully asleep. There was no doubt that Jan was exceedingly proud of her two children. She coaxed me for compliments about them. Given that it was only a matter of minutes since knowing of their existence, I struggled and only just managed to say something positive with some unease.

Jan was indeed a live wire and chatted incessantly. I wondered if it was from a sense of nervousness or anxiety that she felt. Enlightenment was not far away.

'I gather your husband works in Kwang-Ju, Jan. Does he specialise in any particular aspect of law?'

'No, he does everything. He is so clever. He knows everything about law and everyone knows about him. But I'm so sad that I hardly see him.'

'Why? Does he come home very late?'

'Well, the truth is that he…hardly comes home at all. I'm lucky if I see him twice a week.'

119

This statement took me aback. 'Does he work overnight at the office?'

It was not unusual for Koreans to spend the night at the workplace, as I had discovered with my own job. There were often the signs of someone having slept on my desk, files in a muddle, spilt drink marks on the tabletop, and rubbish thrown around the office floor, all things that had to be accepted. The explanation that Jan provided me with was beyond my comprehension. More to the point, I was surprised to hear something so personal spoken of so openly at our very first getting-to-know-each-other meeting.

'My husband has another apartment where he spends most of his time. Sometimes, he comes home after work to see the children, but he spends most of his nights on his own. He likes to meditate.'

While normally I would simply have suppressed my curiosity and not pried any more, I felt that Jan was asking me to interrogate her further, as she wished to let me know her story. 'Can't he meditate here?'

'He says it's too difficult with the noise of the children. And Kate, he really is a very devout Buddhist and likes a very simple lifestyle. He believes in abstinence so he says that it is better for him to be away from me and temptation. Yet he is so generous towards me and the children. He wants us to have everything that we need. His private apartment has none of the comforts we have in this home. It's very simple, and he has a stone bed that he sleeps on. He wants so very much to atone for his sins and misdemeanours and he does not want to impose his behaviours on us… So that's why he has different living arrangements for himself, but he is such a good father and a good husband, Kate. Look at all the things he allows me to have,' she remarked, waving her arm to show the wealth of her possessions. 'He lets me have as much money as I would like for myself and the children. But of course, I am sad that I can't see him every day. Still, I'm lucky to have such a kind and considerate husband.'

I realised that Jan wanted to share her sadness with me. She also wished for my opinion of her rather unusual lifestyle.

'Jan, I must confess that I'm rather surprised by this arrangement. If he was this way inclined, why did he bother to get married? He would certainly have been better off single.' I regretted making this judgemental remark but was promptly provided with a logical rationale.

'In Korea, things are different, you know. We are all expected to get married and have children, even if we don't wish to. I think he felt a lot of pressure from his family to marry and have children. I know life is very different for you, Kate, but in Korea, it is important for every man to have at least one male child. Now his parents and mine are both happy that we have a boy at last. I know you have a boy and a girl but if both your children were girls, would your parents be unhappy about it?'

'No, Jan. It's quite immaterial to us, and many couples opt to not have any children at all. I can see that the social pressures are very high here. Personally, I would find that difficult to cope with but I suppose you grow up to accept these expectations.'

The morning's conversation concluded with a discussion of social norms surrounding marriage and family life. Jan was very persistent about how I would respond to the type of situations that faced her. She wanted that non-Korean perspective on life, something to justify the way she was feeling about her own life. We arranged to meet the following week. I had by now noticed that routine was an important aspect of Korean life. Even friends met routinely on set days of the week.

'Kate, how did you cope with your children when they were little?' I feel so bored with having to look after them all the time. My family is too far away to help me with them… I have so many friends that I go out with but I don't feel able to confide in them. That's why I enjoy being with you.'

We talked about that feeling of entrapment that all mothers must surely feel. Jan's questions, however, were crafted to lead into something explosive for our newfound friendship.

'Do you know what tae kwon do is? It's Korean martial arts. It's so good for keeping fit, I go to classes three times a week.' Jan paused for what seemed like a minute or two and then, keeping her eyes focused on mine, she carried on. 'I have fallen in love, Kate. I am so madly in love with my tae kwon do teacher… I am so worried about being unfaithful to my husband… Tell me, Kate, what would you do in my situation? Would you have an affair even if you had a good husband as I have?'

'How far have you gone, Jan? You say you are in love, but are you actually in a relationship with your teacher? Has he reciprocated your feelings, for example?'

'Oh, we are so much in love, Kate. But he is only twenty years old. I'm eight years older than him. He means everything to me and I want to be with him all the time. Here, I've got a photo of him.' She reached into her wallet and produced a passport-sized headshot with great pride. 'Don't you think he looks handsome in his army uniform?'

I agreed politely and was once again confronted with the question of what I would do in her shoes. 'Jan, I come from a different cultural background. What I would or could do would be very different to choices available to you.'

Jan looked at me with a tear in her eye. 'Do you know, Kate, I have had sex with my husband only on two occasions. Each time I got pregnant, and now that we have a son, my husband has nothing more to do with me. I want a sexual relationship, but I know that I will never again be having sex with my husband for the rest of my life. Since we now have two children, that is proof in my society that we have a fortunate marriage.'

This astounding revelation, plus the fact that Jan had confided something so personal to me on our second meeting, unsettled me deeply. The sadness she was feeling was understandable, but was this deep-rooted unhappiness within her marriage pushing her in the wrong direction? She was unhappy and frustrated, but an affair with a twenty-year-old martial arts teacher did not sound right to me. It could spell ruin for her. Jan was so desperate for love and affection that she would have dropped into anyone's arms. And the more she told me about the man, the more I feared.

'We spent last night together, Kate. You know, he is so poor he does-n't even have an apartment. He lives in a tent, but I didn't mind that. He is trying very hard to earn enough money to start up his own busi-ness. Being with him is all that matters to me, and I feel so happy when I am with him.'

I was digesting every word Jan said to get a fuller picture. It was ev-ident that this affair had been going on for a while and I imagined it was all the uncertainty surrounding her future with this man that had spurred her to enlist me as a friend cum advisor. To discuss this with a Korean would be far too dangerous.

I decided to refocus on Jan's husband's strange behaviour first. 'Jan, I'm not too sure about what you've told me about your husband's be-haviour. Are you sure that he isn't having an affair with someone?'

'Kate, I'm absolutely sure. My husband is an honourable man and he would never do anything like that to me. That's why I feel so guilty about my behaviour. Please give me some advice.'

I felt I was in no position to dispute the trust that she had in her husband, even though I felt very strongly that he was cheating on her. I thought back to how Jan had introduced herself to me, how she had boasted about her wealth. She would have adopted this same approach with her teacher, buying friends, buying lovers. It did not look healthy to me. Why would a twenty-year-old wish to go out with a woman en-cumbered with two little children? Jan was not in any way a beauty, al-though she was lively and fun to be with. I had serious doubts about this young man's motivations, but had to be careful of how I would present things to Jan.

'Jan, I hope that you have not brought your lover into your home. You know that people will talk and your husband could find out. That would mean serious trouble unless you are prepared to give up every-thing you have for a twenty-year-old. I don't imagine he'd be able to support you and, furthermore, how sincere is he?'

'I do understand all those problems, Kate, and I will never bring him here. We always meet in his tent.'

'For the moment, Jan, my advice to you is to never let him know where you live and do not on any account lend him any money.'

Jan swore that she would observe my advice, and we parted, having made a date for our next meeting. This was going to take place earlier than planned.

A few days later, being exhausted from work, I decided to bed down early, only to be woken up by the ringing of the phone. Thoroughly irritated, I looked at the time; it was around half-past three in the morning. I became alarmed. Hardly anyone rang me. And who on earth would call at such an ungodly hour? I picked up the phone.

'Hello, hello, is that you, Kate? I have a serious problem, Kate.' It was Jan. 'I am in shock. I can't believe it, my boyfriend came this night and asked me for money. He had a gun with him and he said that if I didn't give him the money, he would tell my husband about us. What can I do, Kate? Can you come to my place tomorrow morning? Please come. I need someone to talk to,' wailed Jan. Her voice was high-pitched and distinctly distracted, indicating a high level of agitation.

I was rather upset that she had let her lover know where she lived, especially as she had promised me. Still, what was done was done.

'Jan, you promised me that you would not let him know where you lived or what your husband earned. I wish you had listened to me, I have to start work at noon tomorrow – well, that's today, isn't it? So I can see you before I head to work. Will you be all right staying in the apartment tonight?'

'Yes, yes, I'm okay, just very upset. I can't believe what has happened tonight. I'll tell you everything when I see you, Kate. Please don't forget to come.'

It was useless trying to get back to sleep after that, so I pottered around, had a cup of tea, then breakfast around seven before making my way to Jan's place around nine in the morning. It horrified me to see what a disaster she looked. We sat down and she related to me what had happened step by step. How much she omitted or made up, I would never know.

'How did you get rid of him in the end?'

'I gave him forty thousand won that I had in the apartment. He wanted more, but that was all I had with me. But Kate, he said that he wants a hundred thousand won to keep quiet. If I don't give him the money, he will tell my husband everything.' Jan was sniffling and blowing into a paper tissue. Her cheeks were swollen and her eyes bloodshot.

'And have you thought about whether you are going to give it to him or risk your husband finding out?'

'I don't know what to do, Kate. Please tell me what to do.'

'Jan, you realise that this will not stop with the hundred thousand won. He will keep asking for more. That is what blackmailers do! Perhaps you shouldn't give him the money and see what happens next. Who knows, perhaps he won't find your husband. Take a chance and see.'

'Yes, I might do that.'

I gave Jan a big hug. I had no more time to spare. Work beckoned.

'I'll call you later tonight when I get home,' I said as I took leave of her.

It was just before midnight when I called her. The night had thankfully been uneventful, but Jan was still uptight and highly concerned. I advised her to keep a low profile, not go out, and not answer the door to anyone.

Another night of calm, and then the panic started. I had yet another call around four in the morning. I had to once again see Jan before leaving for work.

'Kate, my boyfriend came last night with the gun again.'

'Jan, why did you open the door to him?'

'He threatened me, Kate. He said that he would shoot at the door and open it. I had another forty thousand won that I gave him and he said that he would be back for the rest. He wants one hundred and fifty thousand won now, but something else happened after he had left, Kate. There was another knock at the door and when I opened it, there was a woman outside. She said that she was my husband's mistress, and she demanded that she wanted my husband because she loved him so much. I can't believe what is happening in my life, Kate. What was I to say to her? She says that she has been living with my husband for the last three years and she wants to marry him.'

'Well, I didn't think that your husband being away was for reasons of piety, Jan ,and I think you knew that as well. Perhaps this might be a good trade-off for you. Your husband has been cheating on you all these years. Use it to your advantage. You can ask your tae kwon do teacher to bugger off and try his gun on someone else and inform the police about his behaviour. But what you really have to deal with is your husband and his infidelity. I'm not in a position to advise you as I don't know how Koreans view separation and divorce, so go and see a good lawyer and make sure that he gets a good deal for you and the children.'

The night had no doubt been climactic and shocking for Jan, but in many ways, it created a way out for her. Once again, I had to rush off to work, but at least I could leave her with something more positive and constructive to think about.

We met up a week later in a coffee shop nearby. I was taken aback at how calm and collected Jan was after all the recent events. She acted as though nothing had taken place over the past two weeks; it was surreal. I almost felt as though I had been living through a dream. Our friendship continued until it was time for me to leave her country. She expressed unbound sadness that I was soon to depart and then did not turn up to bid goodbye to me as she had promised. I felt very much that I was no longer a part of Jan's current life; I belonged to her past, already forgotten. It provided me with some rationale that explained Jan's recent aura of calm. I wondered how many affairs Jan had already had. Perhaps it was how she entertained herself in a life that was otherwise fraught with boredom.

Escorted to Death

'Hurry up, Gertie. We've got heaps to do. Your dilly dallying is not going to get us through the day, is it?' Bianca, better known as Binky, was already buckling herself up in the driver's seat of the slightly battered Volkswagen, which was desperately in need of a good wash and wax.

'I'm coming, Binky, I'm coming,' cried out Gertrude as she hurried down the drive and jumped into the passenger seat.

Bianca had already started the engine, and they took off down the bumpy dirt track that led to the road. They turned left, heading for Colchester.

Gertrude and Bianca were twins. Neither had married and, now aged forty-five, they lived together in their parental home, which had once been Watson's Farm. The farm was decidedly too much of a burden for the two women to manage after the death of their father. They sold the land and livestock to their neighbour, Farmer Green, while retaining the cottage and a small allotment surrounding their residence. It was a mutually beneficial deal.

The local villagers were a bit surprised that both girls had remained single. They had been good-looking in their prime and still were; and decidedly intelligent as well. Age had given them a graceful demeanour. Being identical twins, it was difficult to tell them apart barring a few giveaway signs such as their voices, a slight difference in hair colour, and their style of dress. Binky was by far the more organised and decisive of the two.

It was a half-hour drive to Colchester, so Gertie made herself comfortable in her seat. They passed the entrance to Farmer Green's property, waving to him perched on his tractor at the far end. His cows were grazing across the road, also part of his farm. The daffodils were in bloom along the roadside, their vivid yellow contrasting with the lush green carpet of grass. All in all, it was a fabulous summer's day, with a bit of sunshine and a host of wildflowers that would lend anyone a spring to their step.

The two women made this trip every fortnight to stock up on their food supplies generally, all the things that they could not acquire locally. It made a pleasant break from the work week and had become more of an outing rather than a dutiful shopping chore. Lunch in Colchester was usually on the cards but not today; they had a big evening ahead and would have to busy themselves preparing a super dinner for three to entertain their visitor

Gertie rummaged in her handbag and pulled out a rather lengthy shopping list. There were two parts to it. One comprised the usual items that they purchased, and the other was what they planned to get for the night's supper.

'Mm, Dover sole, baby potatoes, spinach, mushrooms. It all sounds so good. I'm getting rather hungry looking at this list. Perhaps we should stop off for a coffee and a cake before we do the shopping, just in case I feel faint with hunger.' Gertie was obsessive about food.

'That sounds like an excellent idea, Gertie. Shall we try that new coffee shop we spotted last week? The cakes and pastries in there looked fabulously scrumptious,' said Binky as she veered left into the turnoff for Colchester. 'You know, we still haven't decided about pudding. We were playing around with chocolate blancmange or syllabub. Any thoughts on that? We'll need to get some ingredients while we're here.'

'I'm all for syllabub. You know it's my favourite, and I'd be happy to make it. So shall we say that's settled?' remarked Gertie while making a quick note of what had to be purchased.

'Yes, syllabub it is then,' said Binky 'and you, dear sister, will make it on our return.'

'Well, that's settled then,' chirped Gertie, happy at getting her way.

'On second thoughts, not everyone likes syllabub. Pperhaps we should go with the blancmange…just in case,' remarked Binky.

'How about we make both? That way, I can still enjoy my syllabub,' piped in Gertie.

'All the same to me, as long as you make both, Gertie,' said Binky.

Gertie not only loved cooking, she was rather fond of eating as well, and Binky was more than happy to indulge in the never-ending recipes that Gertie would try her hand at. Good food was something they both enjoyed.

They had arrived at Sainsbury's car park; it was simply a matter of finding a suitable spot. Binky was always particular about that, wanting to be close to the lifts or the ramp leading to the shops. Gathering their shopping bags together, the two sisters walked down the High Street, eager to try the newest coffee shop in town.

The aroma of fine teas could never compete with the overwhelming smell of fine coffee and home baking. Yet, when it came down to taste, it was tea that the two women relished the most. Gertie decided on an apple and almond flan while Binky went for a blueberry Danish pastry. They would always choose different items from the menu and then share.

'This is absolutely divine,' said Gertie, as she cut half of her flan in two and slid a piece onto Binky's plate.

Binky reciprocated. For a good five minutes, the two were engrossed in simply enjoying their cakes and tea.

'I do hope Hugo is going to enjoy the evening with us,' said Binky, in a thoughtful kind of mood. 'It's been a while since we last saw him. He's such a charmer, no wonder the ladies fall for him! I bet he's in high demand.'

'He certainly is charismatic, no denying that. I'm almost certain that he'll like the fish we've planned on, Binky, so put your worries aside. He did say that he loved fish and we can't get any better than the fishmonger here in Colchester. They say he's the best for miles around.'

'Yes, you're right. I shouldn't keep worrying. Anyway, changing the subject, you did well with those outfits you ordered for us, Gertie. I simply adore them and I'm sure that Hugo will too. How on earth did you find that outlet?' queried Binky

'Oh, it only took a little searching and comparing on the web. I'm only glad that the sizes fit us so perfectly. We make such a picture together in them. Perhaps we should ask Hugo to take one of us together, or better still, one with all three of us, him in the middle of course. I'm sure he'd manage to organise that easily enough.'

'Oh yes! That really would be something to reminisce about in years to come,' retorted Binky with a romantic sigh.

'Shall we then?' remarked Gertie, noting that Binky had taken her last sip of tea.

The coffee shop was abuzz with people waiting for seats when they left.

They had a busy day of shopping and cooking ahead of them. A quick walk through the aisles of Sainsbury and they had their trolley load of the usual things that they purchased except for a few specialities for the evening. It was quickly unloaded into the boot of the car before trekking off to the fishmongers.

Trade was busy. It gave the two women time to look at the tremendous variety on display.

'Binky, look at those oysters! They look fabulous. I know we aren't keen on them, but I recall Hugo mentioning how much he loves them. Shall we get a few just for him?'

'Yes, why not? Let's get some. After all, it's a special night for all of us, so let's make the most of it.'

They purchased a kilo of Dover sole and half a dozen oysters and decided on half a kilo of prawns as well, before leaving the fishmongers. It was going to be a veritable feast, and both sisters hoped dearly that Hugo was going to enjoy it as much as they would. They made a quick detour to the bottle shop for some champagne, wine, and port for afters, and it was back in the car, heading homewards to a very busy afternoon.

By the time the cooking was finished, Binky and Gertie felt exhausted and famished. A quick fruit salad of berries from the garden and a strong cup of tea provided the much-needed pick-me-up. It was such a lovely afternoon, even Fuzzy the cat was having a snooze on one of the garden chairs while butterflies of every hue hovered around, moving gently from flower to flower. The two women could not have dreamed of moving away from this idyllic country hideaway, so far removed from a busy suburban sprawl of houses where neighbours could just look over the fence to see everything that happened next door. That was certainly not for them. They counted their lucky stars they could hold on to what they treasured most in life, their privacy and a quiet life.

The clock was ticking.

Binky went inside the kitchen and reappeared with two glasses of champagne. 'Here's to tonight,' she said. 'We want this to be the best evening ever and that's just what it's going to be,' she said, handing a glass to Gertie.

What better way to start the evening off! The champagne was drunk rather hastily; they needed time to get into their fancy outfits that came with matching tie-around dress coats. Gertie's was blue and Binky's was green. Both looked bewitching with their black silk tights. The women often dressed in lookalike outfits as they had done in their childhood days. It was now simply a case of waiting.

All spruced up, the two women relaxed until they heard the screech of tyres at the front door. It was just a few minutes before six; as always, Hugo was so punctual.

Binky had decided that she would be the one to open the door and show him in while Gertie would wait in the sitting room beside the little trolley that held the drinks and champagne for the evening.

'Hugo, how lovely to see you after all these months,' remarked Binky. 'We have missed you so much. Do come in and make yourself comfortable. Gertie is simply dying to see you.'

Hugo kissed Binky on each cheek. 'My word, you are looking rather well. I must say I have missed you, as much as I hope you've missed me.'

Hugo was ushered into the sitting room, where he received a most joyous welcome from Gertie.

'Hugo, I have missed you so much. How long has it been now since we last saw you? Almost four months, I believe,' said Gertie. 'Yes, that's right, four months or a little over. Do tell us about all your adventures. You said that you were off to the south of France on that wine tasting tour. How was it?'

'Superb, Gertie, just superb,' replied Hugo after having given Gertie a couple of pecks as well. 'One must give credit to the French. They do know their wines. Let's see now, you seem to have got some rather nice champagne here… Hm, pink as well. I do love the pinks. They give such a warm feel to the drink,' replied Hugo, examining the bottle carefully.

Gertie passed the drinks around, and they made a toast to celebrate.

'Ladies, that cooking smells divine. I hope it won't be long before we start tucking into it. I'm developing a rather roaring appetite with that fantastic aroma wafting out of the kitchen.'

'We have some oysters just for you, Hugo,' said Gertie, as they sat around the dining table a few minutes later. 'I think we'll let you tuck into them first before the main course.' She placed the platter of oysters and a little container of lemon butter sauce in front of an ecstatic Hugo.

The two women sat facing him, entranced by the gusto with which he devoured them. They were happily relishing their champagne, looking forward to the main course and dessert. In due course, an exquisite home-cooked meal was wiped clean off the plates.

'That, ladies, is one of the best feasts that I have had in a long time. Who needs to go to France for good food when it is right here on my doorstep?' Hugo knew how to flatter the two women to bits. 'I might just nip upstairs to the toilet while the two of you enjoy the clearing up,' he said. 'I know I'll only get in the way of it all, anyway.' Hugo knew his way around the house.

'We'll see you upstairs in a little while,' piped Binky with a little wink aimed at Gertie.

The women were fastidious about cleaning up thoroughly, but they were also quick with it. With a nifty wipe of the hands with the tea towel, the aprons came off, and they hurried upstairs to get ready for Hugo.

He was going to be in for such a surprise! Both women were giggling as they took their dress coats off to expose their next layer of clothing; one in green, the other in blue. It was erotic underwear. And what had appeared to be black silk tights were in fact black silk stockings held up with black lace garters. They were delighted with how they looked and twirled around in front of the mirror, complimenting each other, and masquerading in naughty and inviting poses.

'Binky, Hugo is really going to love this,' whispered Gertie. The bathroom was only two doors away, and they did not want him to hear them.

'I'll be damned if he doesn't. I mean, just look at us! We couldn't look any sexier, could we?' commented Binky.

It was one more round in front of the mirror, and the two women fell into the luxuriously made bed. Binky had made this her labour of love, a deep blue satin cover with lots of multicoloured satin cushions. It felt like heaven lying on it. The two sisters held hands as they both went into their separate worlds of imagination. How would Hugo react to seeing them? Would he go absolutely wild and jump in with them? Would he say anything and, if so, what? The questions passed through each of their minds.

'Gertie,' said Binky in a soft voice. 'Isn't Hugo taking rather a long time in the bathroom?'

'Hm, I suppose so. How long has he been, then?'

'Almost half an hour. I think we'd better go and see what's going on,' said Binky as she shot up from her reverie. Something didn't seem quite right.

Both girls scrambled out of the bed, leaving it looking rather dishevelled. They ran down the hall and started knocking on the bathroom door.

'Hugo, are you all right? We're just a little worried about you.'

There was no answer. There was alarm on the women's faces as they looked at each other. They tried again; no response. The panic set in.

'Shall I open the door?' asked Gertie of her sister.

Binky gave her the all-clear with a nod. 'Hugo, we're a wee bit concerned about you not answering. We're going to open the door and come in,' she said, as she turned the handle.

Both women gasped and put their hands to their mouths in horror as they saw poor dear Hugo lying face down on the bathroom floor. The awful odour of fishy puke hit them hard in the face. Their immediate reaction was to try not to breathe. Hugo had been sick all over the floor, and there was still a small trickle of saliva dripping out of his mouth. His eyes were closed and his face looked as white as chalk.

'Hugo, speak to us,' said Binky, as she tried to shake a response out of him.

There was no response, no movement.

'Hugo, are you all right? We'll get you to a doctor, don't worry. Gertie, help me turn Hugo round, will you?'

They managed to get him lying on his back. It was not a pretty sight. The bathroom floor was covered in volumes of puke and he looked far from alive.

Gertie broke into uncontrollable tears. 'Oh, Binky! Look at Hugo. I don't believe he's alive, do you? I think Hugo's died on us, leaving us in all this silly, stupid underwear. And he never even got to see us in it!' She tried desperately to feel for a pulse on Hugo's wrist.

Binky had gone ashen white while she watched her sister try one wrist and then the next. No luck.

'It must have been that fish. No! We all ate the fish, so we should be sick too. Oh, Binky, it must have been the oysters. He's the only one who ate the oysters. Let's call Doctor Perkins,' said Gertie as she tried to leave the room to get to the phone.

'No, Gertie. We can't call Doctor Perkins. Don't you see the predicament we are in? We, two longstanding and respectable young women from the village, having an escort for a threesome! No. We most definitely can't call doctor Perkins. Our reputation will be in tatters and we'd never be able to live it down for the rest of our lives. We'll have to think of some other way, something a little more creative.'

Binky rose slowly, went to the basin, and ran the tap; both girls washed their hands and scrubbed up. Gertie was still sobbing.

'Now, Gertie, calm down. Try not to be so emotional. We have a dead body on our hands. An escort, for that matter. We must in no way be associated with him. So how are we to get out of this mess? Put your thinking cap on and we'll have to try and get him out of here, but where to?'

'How can we get out of such a mess? We are responsible for his death. We fed him oysters that were off,' wailed Gertie.

'Hush now, Gertie. You've made a slight mistake there. We bought the oysters from the fishmonger. It's him who's to blame for poor Hugo dying, not us, Gertie.' Binky was always very level-headed. She grabbed a towel and wiped Gertie's tears away and let her have a good blow to clear her nose.

The two women made their way into the bedroom and sat down on the bed, holding hands.

'It's time to think now, Gertie. We must not be associated in any way with Hugo, so we need to get him away from the cottage. But where to is the big question. We could leave him somewhere along the roadside I suppose? Oh, don't forget we need to get rid of his car as well, so we'll have to drive his car, and ours as well, so that we can get back home.'

A plan was hatched. The two women quickly climbed into their gardening clothes, pulling them over their fancy underwear. And then the hard work started. Binky grabbed Hugo by his feet, and Gertie had him under his arms. It was a slow climb down the stairs, then into the garden. Getting Hugo into his car was a challenge, but they finally had him propped up in the passenger seat. Binky decided it best that she drive his car while Gertie would follow her in theirs. Thankfully, there were no street lights. The wind had picked up and the lightest of rain beat down on their cheeks.

'Who was that?' shrieked Gertie, just as she was about to get into the driver's seat. She jumped back, only to tread on poor Fuzzy's tail.

'You're getting jittery for nothing, Gertie. Stay calm and do as I say. There's no one out at this time of night. Are you ready? Just follow me.'

They drove slowly. No headlights, not until they reached the main road, anyway. Once again, they were heading on the road towards Colchester, but this time, they would take a detour into Church Lane. That was the next left. It was very much an old country road dotted with potholes. The drive was arduous. Binky had to either pull Hugo towards her or push him away from her, depending on the bumps.

The little church was soon visible, and Binky sighed with relief. They had decided that they would park Hugo's car, with him inside, beside the church. That way, hopefully, he would be found first thing in the morning and, all going to plan, he'd be taken care of sooner rather than later.

There was a sharp jerk as Binky jammed on the brakes. She was not used to driving such a posh car; it had rattled her a bit, and she almost fell out of the driver's seat.

Gertie drove up alongside and Binky jumped into the passenger seat, relieved to be away from a very dead Hugo.

'Carry straight on, Gertie. We can turn down Potter's Lane and get home that way. I want to be away from this place as fast as I can,' wailed Binky, finally feeling the full force of the night's events.

Gertie reached out and patted her on the hand. The two sisters always stood by each other, whatever the situation. They both knew it would be a long night of scrubbing and cleaning.

'I hope no one saw us…or heard the car…' remarked Gertie.

'No, I believe we have indeed been very lucky.'

It was a sleepless night even after the cleaning was over. Binky, as always, took charge of the situation, reminding Gertie to act as normal as possible the next day. They both had the day off work, and just as well; it would give them time to compose themselves. Yet neither could get much done, try as they did. It was seemingly endless cups of tea. They listened to the local news; the vicar had discovered the parked car with Hugo, but nothing further was divulged.

The late evening news gave more information about the body being found, and the possible cause of death being food poisoning. The sisters heaved a sigh of relief. It appeared as though the whole thing would blow over. On Friday, both girls would be at work, and people were bound to talk about the strange events. They would have to do their best, to pretend interest but no knowledge about what might have happened. Gossip was always flapping around; no one tired of it. They got through that day and finally felt able to relax with a glass of champagne on Friday evening. It was a late night after their favourite quiz show, and life was back to normal.

Saturday dawned bright and beautiful. Gertie was hanging the washing out in the back garden when she heard the knock on the front door. Binky answered. Two cops stood outside.

'Colchester constabulary, ma'am. This is Sergeant Black. I'm Sergeant Robertson. May we come in to ask you a few questions regarding a recent death in your area?'

'Yes…yes, of course,' said Binky, opening the door wider. She felt the blood drain from her head; it took immense willpower to maintain her composure. 'Do come in, take a seat. I'll just go and get my sister… she's hanging the washing… I…I suppose you'd want to speak to both of us?' muttered Binky as she dashed out; it afforded her the time she needed to gather her thoughts together, and she'd have to calm Gertie before they faced the cops.

Anyway, what did it have to do with them? Nothing. The cops were just questioning everyone in the neighbourhood. Standard procedure, pure and simple!

'Gertie, it's best you let me do the talking. Just sit there and be polite and smile at them. I'm sure it's just the usual door-to-door.'

'So, it's Ms Gertrude and Ms Bianca Watson. Sisters, I gather?'

'Yes, that's right,' said Binky. 'We've lived here all our lives.'

'Well, I'm sure you've heard about the body that was found in a car by St Augustine's church… We're just wondering if either of you saw or heard anything on Wednesday evening, say between the hours of nine and midnight?'

'No…no, I don't believe so. It certainly has shocked the neighbour-hood, though. I wonder what he was doing by the church, anyway? Seems rather odd,' remarked Binky with a questioning look.

'Yes, it's not often one drives oneself to church to die. You weren't by any chance expecting a visitor that evening?'

'No, not at all. We live a very quiet life here, and I believe Gertie and I retired rather early that night. Wednesdays are usually an early night for us.'

'You don't perhaps know anyone by the name of Hugo Bertram?'

'No…no, I don't. That is, we don't,' remarked Binky.

The cop redirected the question to Gertie, who reaffirmed in the negative.

'Should you remember anything that you might have seen or heard over the past few days, anything that seemed out of the ordinary, please get in touch with us. We feel that there is a particular connection with this parish, so we'll more than likely be back for another chat.'

They took their leave, looked curiously around the side of the prop-erty, and drove off.

The sisters went inside and sat down on the sofa.

'It's just routine. It must be, but I feel that those coppers have some-thing on us,' remarked Binky. 'Put the kettle on, Gertie. I need an extra-strong cuppa. I feel completely drained.'

The cops did not look back until they had got into their vehicle.

'There's something odd about those two women, Black. I almost feel that they are somehow connected with this affair. It's good we didn't mention that the body was strangely in the passenger seat.'

The two officers got in their car, cast a suspicious eye back at the house, and then moved on.

'Right, Gertie, I'm off to Colchester. Shan't be too long. In the meantime, you know what needs doing. Let's make this swift,' remarked Binky.

She gave the officers enough time to disappear into the distance be-fore heading into town.

Binky explained to Camille, their travel agent, what they were after. 'Yes, two tickets, please. That's right, Kingston, Jamaica.'

'I can get you both on a flight tomorrow morning if that suits you? So you have an aunty living there? How exciting. Well, I mean, not that she's so seriously sick, but to have a reason to go over to such a paradise... I do hope you get to have some fun while you're over there. No shortage of sunshine anyway, but I would advise you to get yourselves a couple of good brollies. It's an awful lot of rain with that tropical heat.'

'Thank you so much, Camille, and we do so appreciate you taking care of Fuzzy for us. We'll hope to see you when we get back, don't know when, but Aunt Meg would have to be completely well before we leave her. Besides, we certainly intend on having a bit of fun as well.'

Camille was rather taken aback by the unusual destination requested. The sisters had never mentioned an aunt in Jamaica.

Binky got back to the house in high spirits. 'We leave tomorrow, Gertie, in the morning. Isn't it wonderful! It's just what the two of us need. A clean break to forget all this dreadful business.'

'Tell me all, Binky. I can't wait to get away from here right now. Tomorrow morning sounds perfect...and I've got the bags packed with everything.'

'Let's not forget a couple of brollies. Camille said that it's awfully wet out there. It's that tropical weather and the monsoons, you see...'

The next morning, the taxi picked the girls up at eight-thirty and two very relieved and excited women chatted excitedly about their imaginary aunt and a well-deserved, open-ended holiday as their cab raced them on to Heathrow.

'Come and take a look at this, Black,' said Robertson. 'This report says that Hugo Bertram worked as an escort for that agency in town, the one called Utopia. Furthermore, on the night in question, Wednesday, our man Hugo was booked in for an appointment, and guess where? At none other than Watson's Farm, with those two bloody women! Who would have guessed? Two respectable women in a sleepy little village, booked in for a threesome and all! And the agency says that Bertram never made contact after that engagement.' Black burst out laughing and was still ripping his sides as Robertson dragged him towards their car.

'Those two women had everything to do with Bertram's death. I mean, if it was food poisoning, why didn't they call the doctor? They didn't, because they murdered him, perhaps to rob him. Who knows? But we'll jolly well nail them.'

The police car sped on towards the village, only barely avoiding a collision with a taxi going in the opposite direction, and distinctly over the speed limit as well.

'What's a taxi doing around here?' remarked Black. 'One doesn't see taxis in this backwater? What's the world coming to these days?'

'Indeed! Good question… You know, Black, that's about the most sensible thing you've said in the past week.'

Robertson and Black had just pulled up at the now-empty Watson residence.

Binky and Gertie were just about to take off on their plane.

'Binky, do you think that we are in any way liable for Hugo's… Hugo's demise?'

'Well, technically, they could prove that to be the case if they find out our connection with him, and they surely will, once they identify him.'

'What a good idea this holiday is!' Gertie sighed contentedly as the plane took off.

www.ingramcontent.com/pod-product-compliance
Lightning Source LLC
Chambersburg PA
CBHW051231210726
48290CB00003B/910